Waltham Forest Libraries

Please return this item by the last date stamped. The loan may be
renewed unless required by another customer.

Feb 2020		

D0532884

Need to renew your books?
http://www.walthamforest.gov.uk/libraries or
Dial 0333 370 4700 for Callpoint – our 24/7 automated telephone renewal
line. You will need your library card number and your PIN. If you do not
know your PIN, contact your local library.

Here
in the
Real
World

SARA PENNYPACKER

HarperCollins *Children's Books*

First published in the United States of America by HarperCollins Publishers in 2020
Published simultaneously in Great Britain by HarperCollins *Children's Books* in 2020
HarperCollins *Children's Books* is a division of HarperCollins*Publishers* Ltd,
HarperCollins Publishers
1 London Bridge Street
London SE1 9GF

The HarperCollins website address is
www.harpercollins.co.uk
1

ISBN 978–0–00–837169–2

Waltham Forest Libraries

904 000 00667423	
Askews & Holts	07-Feb-2020
STO	£7.99
6254733	

To my daughter, Hillary,
for keeping this book here in the real world

one

Ware patted the two bricks stacked beside him on the pool deck, scored on the morning's ramble. Tomorrow he'd bash them into chips to build the ramparts of his castle, but tonight he had another use for them.

He swirled his legs through the water, turquoise in the twilight, and at exactly 7:56, he snapped on his goggles and adjusted them snug. "The boy began to prepare himself for the big event." He whispered the voice-over, in case anyone had their windows open, or the Twin Kings were lurking around.

The Twin Kings weren't twins, just two old men who dressed alike in plaid shorts and bucket hats. They weren't kings either, but they paraded around Sunset

Palms Retirement Village like royal tyrants, making life miserable for anyone they encountered.

Ware had studied the Middle Ages in school. Back then, kings could be kind and wise, kings could be cruel and crazy. Luck of the draw: serf or knight, you lived with it.

The first time the Twin Kings had come across Ware, he'd been cheek down in the grass, watching a line of ants patiently climb up, then over, then down a rock, thinking about how much harder human life would be if people didn't know they could just go around some obstacles. "Space Man" they'd dubbed him, claiming they'd had to yell at him three times before he'd lifted his head.

Now, whenever they found him, they delivered some zinger they found so hilarious they had to double over and grab their knees. The comments were not hilarious, though. They were only mean.

Which was okay—people made fun of him for spacing out; he was used to it.

No, the mortifying thing was when Big Deal came out and sent the kings slinking away with a single glare. An eleven-and-a-half-year-old boy was supposed to protect his grandmother, not the other way around.

"Oh, they're harmless," Big Deal had said last night, laughing and making him feel even more ashamed. "They're deathly afraid of germs, so just tell them you're sick. Diarrhea works best."

As if he'd called them up by thinking of them, the Twin Kings rolled around the corner, hands clasped around their royal bellies. "Earth to Space Man!" the shorter one cackled. "Don't get your air hose caught in the drain down there!"

Ware glanced back at his grandmother's unit, then faced them. "Better stay away. I'm *sick*." He grabbed his belly and groaned in a convincing manner. The Twin Kings scuttled back around the corner.

Ware raised his eyes to the clock again: 7:58. He kicked off the seconds in the water.

At 7:59, he picked up the bricks. Then he slowly filled his lungs with the sunscreeny air—hot and sweet, as if someone was frying coconuts nearby—and slipped into the deep end. The bricks seemed to double in weight, sinking him softly to the bottom.

He'd never been on the bottom before, thanks to a certain amount of padding that functioned as an internal flotation device. "Baby fat," his mother called it. "It'll turn into muscle." Witnessing his bathing-suited self in his grandmother's mirror every day, he realized his mother had omitted a crucial detail: *how* it would turn into muscle. Probably exercise was involved. Maybe tomorrow.

Ware located the four huge date palms—each one anchoring a corner of the pool. Their chunky trunks staggered in the ripples like live gargoyles.

At eight, the twinkle lights winding up those trunks were set to come on. Tonight he would see it from the bottom of the pool. Okay, the big event was not exactly a dazzling spectacle, but he'd discovered that everything looked more interesting through water—mysteriously distorted, but somehow clearer, too. He could hold his breath for over a minute, so he'd have plenty of time to appreciate the effect.

Five seconds later, though—a surprise. The palm fronds began to flash red.

Ware understood right away: ambulance. Three times already in the weeks he'd been at Sunset Palms, he'd been awakened by strobing red lights—no shock in a retirement place. He knew the drill: the ambulance cut the siren at the entrance—no sense causing any extra

4

heart attacks. It parked between the buildings, and then a crew ran around poolside where the doors to the units were sliders, easier to roll the stretchers in, haul the people out.

Don't be afraid, he telegraphed to whoever lay on the stretcher, the way he had the other times. Scared people seemed like raw eggs to him, wobbling around without their shells. It hurt just to think about people being scared.

While he watched the date palms pulse, he thought about being happy instead. How happiness could sneak up on you, like, for instance, when your parents send you away for the summer to your grandmother's place, which you know you'll hate, but it turns out you love it there because for the first time in your life you have long hours free and alone. Well, except for maybe two old men so harmless they're afraid of germs.

An egret, as white and smooth as though carved from soap, glided through the purpling sky. In a movie, a single flying bird like that would let you know that the main character was starting out on a journey. Ware wished, the way he always did when he saw something wonderful, that he could share things like this. *You see that? Wow.* But he didn't really know anyone besides his grandmother here, and she hadn't been feeling well today, had barely stepped out of—

Ware released the bricks, burst to the surface, snapped off his goggles, and saw: Big Deal's sliding glass doors gaping open like a gasp, two EMTs inside, bent over a stretcher.

A third EMT squinted toward the pool, her white coat flashing pink in the lights, as if her heart beat in neon. Mrs. Sauer from Unit 4 hovered behind her, bathrobe clutched to her chest, face clenched. She raised one bony arm like a rifle and aimed her finger right at Ware.

Ware shot over to the ladder, slapped the water from his left ear, his right, and as he scrambled out he heard, "That's her grandson. Off in his own world."

At eight exactly, the twinkle lights came on.

two

Ware woke, disoriented to find himself in his own bed instead of on the prickly couch at his grandmother's place. The night swept over him—the grim, silent ride to the hospital, following the ambulance in Mrs. Sauer's old Buick; the air-conditioned waiting room where he'd shivered, pool soaked and worried, until a nurse dropped a blanket over his shoulders; his mother charging in a few hours later, her jaw set like a rock. He flung off the sheets and got up.

Halfway downstairs, he heard his parents talking in the kitchen.

"Except that's not what you wanted," he heard his father say.

"I know, I know," his mother said. "I only wish . . ."

Ware hurried the rest of the way down. "What do you wish, Mom? Is Big Deal okay?"

His dad slid off the counter. "You all right? Tough night, yesterday."

"Mom. How's Big Deal?"

"She's awake," his mother answered, looking down into her coffee. "She'll be okay."

"Oh, good. So when am I going back?"

"Back?"

His mom's phone rang just then. She picked it up and gripped her forehead with the other hand as if she were afraid it might shatter, and marched into the bedroom.

His father watched her go with a worried expression.

Of course, worried was his dad's normal state. "It comes with the job," he often said, and he always sounded proud of it. Signaling airplanes down the runway meant thinking about every possible catastrophe.

But Ware grew worried then, too. His mother was the manager at the city's crisis center. She juggled twenty volunteers' schedules, talked people down from bridges, and got babies delivered. She *took control*, as if control were a package sitting on the doorstep with her name on it. She didn't grip her forehead as if it might shatter.

"Dad. Big Deal's okay. Mom said. When's she getting out?"

"Well. She is okay, she just let her blood sugar get low yesterday. That's not good with her condition. They'll have to—"

"Her condition? Is Big Deal sick?"

"Oh. Well, it's . . . she's not young. But she fell, is—"

"Being old is a condition?"

"She fell, is the thing. They need to make sure she's all right."

"Oh. Okay, good. So what about the plan?"

"The plan?"

"I spend the summer there, so you and Mom can work double shifts, buy this house. The *plan*."

"Oh. Well, that was plan A," his dad agreed. He picked up a Summer Rec brochure from the counter. "Plan B might be a little different."

three

Ware stood at the kitchen door, forehead pressed to the screen, building his argument.

He could stay home alone, so no, he sure did not need to go to Rec again, if that's what they were thinking. Rec was another name for day care, with heat rash and humiliation thrown in free of charge.

The first time he'd gone to that program had been the summer after first grade, and the memory still hurt. "Go join in with the others," a teenaged counselor had urged.

"I am. Joined in with the others," he'd answered, bewildered.

"No. I mean *inside* the group. You're *outside*."

Ware had studied the situation, trying to see what the counselor saw. He saw something different. He saw a huge space with kids scattered all over. "The outside is part of the inside when it's people," he'd tried to explain, then felt his face burn when that counselor had leaned into another counselor and laughed.

In that precise moment he'd learned that the place that had always felt so right—standing enough apart from a situation that he could observe it, in the castle watchtower, as he'd come to think of it later—was wrong.

Afterward, Ware had tried to forget the embarrassing episode. And that was when he'd learned the cruel irony of memory: you could be *capable* of forgetting things—Ware himself, at six, routinely forgot to comb his hair or bring home his lunch box—but the harder you tried to erase something from your brain, the deeper it got engraved.

The other kids hadn't forgotten either. The *outside* label stuck to him summer after summer, invisible but undeniable, like a bad smell, and *outside* was where they left him.

Which was okay, although from then on, he made certain to appear to be part of the group if any grown-ups were watching. It wasn't hard—"joined in" was simply a matter of geography to grown-ups. A few steps one direction or another did the trick.

No matter. He wasn't going back. Not even for the week or two until he could return to Sunset Palms.

He'd been really happy there. The pool had been barely over his head and so narrow he could practically touch both walls at once. But the instant he'd slipped in, he'd always felt good. Really good. And something about it had worked like fertilizer on his imagination. He'd had dozens of great ideas drifting around that pool. Hundreds.

Even better, when he'd told his grandmother about his report, "Defending Medieval Castles," and how he wanted to actually build a model to see for himself how life had been for the knights, she'd shocked him by waving her hands over her dining table and saying, "Build it right here. We'll eat our meals at the counter, and that's that."

At Sunset Palms, he'd spent entire blissful days exploring the neighborhood, picking up things for his model. Whole nights happily building it. He'd been a little homesick, sure. But something that had been clenched tight inside him his whole life had loosened.

He stepped into the backyard, looking for something to convince his parents that he could keep busy for a week or so. The yard seemed to shrug in apology. "The boy surveyed a wasteland," he voice-overed—silently, of course.

"Wasteland" was an exaggeration, but not much. Mr. Shepard wasn't a spend-money-on-yard-maintenance kind of landlord, and his parents weren't the spend-time-working-on-a-lawn kind of parents, so the yard was barren. Besides an old shed crammed with junk abandoned when the previous tenants left a decade ago, there were only a couple of rusting lounge chairs and a listing picnic table. They seemed to be gasping for final breaths before the weeds drowned them. "Wasteland," he repeated.

Which was, he suddenly realized, exactly *perfect*.

He jumped off the step. A stunningly great idea had just sprung up, even without the imagination-boosting benefit of a pool.

When his parents bought this place at the end of the summer, they'd own the backyard, too. The lounge chairs could be broken down to make armor. The shed would work as a throne room. The picnic table could be a draw-bridge once he sawed off the legs. He'd turn the narrow side yard into a barbicon, the courtyard of deathly obstacles for attackers. No boiling oil, obviously, but definitely a catapult. He'd notch toeholds in the wooden fence and take running leaps to claim the top—mounting the ramparts, it was called. This last was such a satisfying image, he replayed it, this time in classic knight's stance: *Chin up, chest out, advance boldly.*

Ware dropped to the picnic table and stretched out. Sometimes he wished he lived back in the Middle Ages. Things were a lot simpler then, anyway, especially if you were a knight. Knights had a rule book—their code of chivalry—that covered everything: *Thou shalt always do this, thou shalt never be that.* If you were a knight, you knew where you stood.

Too often, Ware wasn't even sure he *was* standing. Sometimes he felt as if he was wafting, in fact. A little drifty.

His mother, like the knights, operated from a clear code, and she was always trying to share it with him. "If you aren't thinking three steps ahead," she would say, for example, "you're already four steps behind." The trouble was, Ware hadn't the faintest clue how to unravel an advice-puzzle like that.

His father lived by a code also, made up of sports sayings. It was equally undecipherable.

"Ware!" his dad called just then from the back door.

Given the level of irritation in his voice, Ware knew he'd called a few times already. He jumped up. "Sorry. What?"

"Inside. Team huddle."

four

Ware's mother sat at the kitchen table, still gripping her phone.

"What happened?"

His dad took a seat. He patted the chair between them.

Ware stayed standing. "What's wrong?"

"When she fell, your grandmother fractured her hips. Both hips!" His mother's voice was extremely cheerful and determined, but it had gone up into a strange new register. "She'll have to have them replaced."

"Replaced?" Images of things that got replaced presented themselves unhelpfully in his mind. Batteries, light bulbs, toothbrushes. A hip didn't fit.

"Artificial joints. Surgery. Nothing for a child to

be concerned with." His mother smiled hard, but she blinked her eyes quickly.

Ware felt the world collapse a little, as if it had suddenly remembered it was hollow at its core. Was his mother going to *cry*?

His dad seemed as shaken as Ware by those blinking eyes. He took over. "Hip replacement is a common operation, and your grandmother is pretty tough."

Pretty tough. Ware almost laughed at that. Big Deal was always asking piercing questions—*She's direct*, his mother explained in excuse—and she expected answers. Whenever they saw her—holidays mostly—she ran the visit like a military maneuver. Even the Thanksgiving turkey had seemed to salute when she walked by. He'd been kind of scared of her, actually.

But staying with her, he'd experienced the flip side of her toughness. Instead of holding it up against him, she'd wrapped it around him like a shield, the way she'd done with the Twin Kings.

"I'll help her out. Do stuff for her when I'm back there next week," he said.

His dad shook his head. "Both hips at the same time means a longer rehab. She won't be able to go home for

17

a while. Probably not this summer. Which means . . ."

Ware's mom straightened. "Don't worry, Ware, I've got your summer all planned out."

Ware saw her brighten with the energizing pleasure schedules always brought her. "No, Mom, please," he tried. Schedules made him feel as if he were being sucked into a pit of tar.

"I'll drop you at the community center on my way to work. You'll take the three forty-five bus home. You'll bring lunch, because we're not paying for the junk they serve there. Now on weekends . . ."

The light seemed to dim over his head. Apparently the city wasn't content with ruining weekdays—they had weekend Rec, too. Weekend Wrecked, more like. His mother was just explaining dinners when he managed a gurgle from the tar pit. "No!"

"Excuse me? No, what?"

"Rec. I want to stay home. Vashon is around until August, and Mikayla is—"

"Ware. You'll go. Now, we'll both stop home for dinner most nights in between shifts, but—"

"I'm old enough to—"

"You're going to Rec. Now, sunscreen before you

leave. SPF eighty at minimum, hypoallergenic, I'll get a case, remember the tops of your ears. Stay hydrated. Now, by mid-July . . ."

Ware looked to his father. His mother made the rules, but sometimes . . .

His father's jaw hung open worshipfully. After fifteen years of marriage, he was still bedazzled by the way his wife could snap into action.

"Dad, please. I'm eleven and a half. Nobody goes that old."

His father tore himself away and refocused on Ware. "We'll make it up to you. How about a new bike? A basketball hoop? Whatever you want. Now, you'll take my big first aid kit—"

"What I want is not to go to Rec. Can I have that?" Ware tried to hide how surprised he was at what he'd just said. His skin felt too tight, as if it didn't fit the reckless version of himself he'd grown into in only three weeks away.

His mom looked pretty surprised, also. She opened her mouth, but nothing came out. The news that her body would betray her like this seemed to bewilder her even more.

Ware watched her go to the sink, squeeze out a sponge, and start wiping the counter, hard.

Then she stopped. She leaned her head against the side of the refrigerator. Ware could tell from the way her back moved that his crisis-center-manager mother, obeyed by babies and bridge jumpers alike, was having a hard time ordering air in and out of her lungs. The sight made Ware's own chest ache.

He got up and wrapped his arms around her waist. She tipped her head and looked down at him for a long time.

Her hair, which she always wore coiled into a tight bun, had come undone. A strand dangled over the toaster. The toaster wasn't on, and his mother's hair wasn't metal, of course, but Ware had inherited his father's worrying nature. That wet sponge . . .

He sneaked a hand out and unplugged the cord.

His mother gave him a puzzled look, as if she were trying to place him. Then she smiled as if maybe she remembered. "You," she said, in a voice so soft with compassion that for a second, Ware's hopes surged.

"I'm sorry," she sighed. "But with making sure your grandmother's okay and working double shifts, we can't be worrying about you, too. Being alone all day."

"Worrying about you being safe," his dad added.

"We need to know you're . . ." His mother picked up the Rec brochure and consulted it. "Spending your time having Meaningful Social Interaction with other kids." She clipped the brochure to the fridge with a click that sounded final. "Go get ready."

five

Ware hadn't spoken a word the whole ride to the community center.

Over the years, he'd argued the point too many times already: He had plenty of Meaningful Social Interaction at school. Truckloads full. He had friends—Vashon and Mikayla. And by the way, why did she always act as if two wasn't enough?

But sometimes he wanted to spend time alone. Sometimes he *needed* to. If that made him a disappointing son, well, couldn't his parents accept their bad luck, having a disappointing son?

But now, standing at the registration desk, Ware wished he'd fought a little. Or a lot. He wished, actually, that he'd opened the car door and rolled out—at slow speed, onto soft grass, of course. He'd seen a kid do that in a movie once. The kid had broken her arm, but it had certainly gotten the mother's attention.

Ms. Sanchez, the Rec director, who always looked as tired as Ware suddenly felt, began reciting the rules. "The community center is not responsible for lost or damaged items; the staff will not administer medicines . . ."

Ware zoned out—five summers he'd heard these rules—and scanned the room.

Nothing had changed. The concrete walls, chipped paint the color of Band-Aids, were hung with the same curling posters: SAVE A LIFE—LEARN THE HEIMLICH!; IDENTIFY POISONOUS SNAKES IN FLORIDA; and oddly, HOW TO MAKE THE PERFECT CUP OF COFFEE.

The floor was marked for the basketball court it used to be, and a hoop still hung at one end, although the basketballs had long ago been replaced with Wiffle balls after some big-muscled kid managed to hurl one through a clerestory window. You could still pick glass out of the floorboards underneath.

In back was the Art Hut, doubly misnamed since it wasn't a hut at all and nothing close to art ever went on there, not if art was something you created yourself instead of "Trace your hand, add a red triangle."

The place sounded just the way he remembered, too: the high-pitched roar of kids establishing the day's alliances or battles.

Most discouraging, the air smelled exactly the same: feet, Lysol, and vaguely but insistently, vomit from legions of little kids staggering inside, tomato-faced after running around under a broiling Florida sun, heaving up lunch. Ware had done it himself. He felt his breakfast shift threateningly in his stomach as he remembered.

He saw only three other kids from his age group— they'd be Elevens this year—two boys and a girl. All three were the kind of kids who found the community center's cavernous space an irresistible acoustic challenge. One of the boys caught his eye and whooped. The other gulped and let out a thunderous burp.

Ware raised his hand to half-mast with a nod, but inside, he felt the familiar contracting retreat of the thing that lived deep in his chest, which must be his soul.

Two weeks into the program, everybody was already knotted up into groups. Only two kids stood alone.

One was a tall boy he'd never seen before, whose

neck rose out of his striped T-shirt like a periscope. After a full 360-degree scan of the room, the boy pretended to study the ant farm on a windowsill. Ware knew he was pretending because the ants had died off, probably out of boredom, a few years ago.

The other was a seven-year-old he thought of as Sad Girl. Sad Girl stood at the door and cried the whole first day she'd come two summers ago. Her silent tears had about killed Ware. Desperate to stop them, he'd swiped the prized unicorn puppet from a couple of older girls and brought it to her, but she'd only pressed it to her side and kept those streaming eyes glued on the door, her lashes clumped together and heavy.

Today Sad Girl was looking mournfully at a lump of Play-Doh on her palm. It was the same pinkish beige as the walls, and even from the registration desk, Ware could see it was crusty. The girl looked up, right at him, as if she had sensed him watching her. She tipped her palm so the clay fell to the floor. Ware nodded in sympathy.

His mom tore out a check, handed it over. "That's for the full summer package—weekends, too."

Ms. Sanchez wrote SUMMER PKG after his name the

way Ware imagined a judge might write SENTENCE: DEATH. "Drop in any time you want. Just sign in at the door so we know the day's head count."

"Oh, he'll be here every—" his mother started to say, but the director had leaped up to pull a kid out of a trash can.

"How much does this cost, Mom?"

"Oh, now, that's not something for a child to worry about."

"I'm not worried. I'll pay you twice as much to let me stay home." This was his new reckless self talking, since there were only forty-six dollars in his shoe box at home, but he was desperate.

"I have to get to work, but I'll see you at dinner." His mother dug into her tote bag. She pulled out a bus pass. "For July. The bus stop is right out front." Then she came up with the first aid kit and a pack of antibacterial wipes. "If you touch anything . . ."

"Mom!"

She zipped the bag closed. "Try to have a good time, okay? Maybe you'll make a friend."

Ware gave up. He tightened his cheeks in something he hoped looked like a smile and nodded. Then he walked over to the cubbies and stuffed the first aid kit and the wipes deep into the back of one. He hung his backpack on a hook, feeling exhausted.

"Elevens!" Ms. Sanchez called from the side door. "Outside with Kyle for Rec-Trek. Tens, you too."

Rec-Trek. Ware had almost forgotten. A dozen times around the building, first walking, then marching and skipping, and finally running at faster and faster speeds, until your head pounded and sweat poured down your back, followed by five circuits of free movement, which wasn't free since you had to keep circling the building. Half an hour of mandatory exercise. A couple of years there'd been kids on crutches and once a boy in a wheel-chair—even they only got to go a little slower. Ware sighed and started for the door.

"This place should have a real playground," he com-plained as he passed the director. He was a little shocked he'd said it out loud, but she seemed too tired to take offense.

"This place should have a lot of things," she agreed with a shrug. "Tell it to my budget."

six

Outside, Ware positioned himself far enough apart from the others that he could study the situation, but close enough that an adult would assume he was enjoying Meaningful Social Interaction.

The tall-necked boy slouched out with the Tens. He scanned the scene, and when his gaze found Ware, he wormed his way over. "I'm Ben. I haven't seen you before. You new here, too?" he asked with an eagerness that reminded Ware of himself his first weeks here. He winced with the recognition.

"No," he answered. "I'm old here."

"Tens behind Elevens, single file," Kyle—this year's counselor—called, and the tall-necked boy drifted back.

Watching him go, Ware realized that he'd described

it exactly—he felt *old* here at the Rec. Until this very moment, he hadn't even known that old was a feeling, had thought it was just a wrinkled, faded way of appearing. But old was a feeling all right. Worn out.

He began to shuffle with the Elevens toward the giant oak at the corner of the property that marked the start of the circuits.

"Trek one, walk!"

Nothing had changed outside, either.

Over the side fence, he saw the pink bell tower of the Glory Alliance Church. Tuesdays, the odor of lasagna wafting out from their kitchen made Rec smell a lot better than usual. Friday afternoons, the air rang with choir practice. Ware liked to imagine that the thunderous hallelujah-ing was the soundtrack to a victory-against-all-odds movie, one that starred him surviving another week.

The Elevens turned the corner into the back parking lot. There, the Grotto Bar's neon sign loomed over the fence, promising IC OLD BEER in blue letters beside a pink flamingo endlessly dipping its beak into a golden mug. Ware had tasted beer, and he couldn't fathom why a human being, let alone a flamingo, would drink it, but he liked that the bar was there, too. On rainy days, colorful streaks rivered down the windows in the Art Hut from that neon sign. *You see that? Wow.*

He stopped, squinting his eyes at the sign, trying to re-create the rain slide of electric colors, until the Tens passed him and he had to run to catch the end of the line.

Rec-Trek's third leg was alongside the city library. It would be to nice spend the day under those cool, dark ceilings, poring over book after book in the quiet. Medieval history had a whole shelf in there.

And then the line of kids, a dozen heads drooping in the heat already, trudged past the front of the community center, heading for the old oak again.

"Trek two, march!" Kyle yelled, like a warden to his prisoners.

The kids around Ware dutifully lifted their knees and surged forward.

But Ware stopped.

Because he was last in line, no one would notice if he slipped behind that tree, skipped a few circuits.

Ware's old obedient self argued with his new reckless self for a few seconds. Then he darted.

Wedged between the massive trunk and the fence,

watching the last of the Tens disappear around the corner, he felt giddy, electrified.

He gripped the limb above his head and swung himself up. Belly to the broad limb, he stretched his arms, his legs. Branching. He imagined sap rushing through his veins, fresh leaves unfurling from his fingers and toes.

He didn't feel old anymore.

Too soon, though, he heard the thud of footsteps coming back around the building. He shimmied out farther into the green, way over the fence now, and closed his eyes in ostrich-logic until they passed.

Then he looked out. And nearly fell from the tree.

Someone had laid siege to the church.

seven

The roof had been torn off, the walls half smashed. Their tops looked like crenellated parapets—he'd learned the term researching for his castle report; it meant notched like a jawbone missing teeth.

Ware dropped from the branch and flew across the overgrown lawn to the front steps.

One of the massive wooden doors had been smashed to splinters, the other lay canted out like a drawbridge half raised. Above his head, an iron pole jutted from the wall. Shards of glass below told Ware that the pole had held a light, but now it cast a pointed shadow down toward the doorway, as if ordering him inside.

Before he obeyed, Ware climbed the front steps and studied the shadow. Castle designers incorporated sundials on south-facing walls like this, public timepieces for the villagers.

He calculated. His mother had left at eight forty-five, so it was about nine now. He had nothing to draw with, but he'd skinned his knee dropping from the tree. Carefully, dipping up blood with his finger, he painted an *I* and an *X* at the tip of the shadow.

Then he scrambled over heaps of wreckage to the bell tower. In the light streaming down from the gaping top, where the spire used to be, a steel stairway winked all the way up like a promise.

Before he could climb, he heard the clink of metal hitting something gritty.

He ducked and peered around.

Through the back doorway, he saw a scrawny girl squatting in the backyard of the church beside a squashed slide. Flat ribbons of yellow hair splayed out under a saggy straw hat. She raised a trowel and stabbed the ground.

In his report, he'd learned the value of observing intruders from above before they saw you. *Battles were won and lost in the watchtower*, he'd written, and Mrs. Sprague had stuck a smiling light-bulb sticker beside the sentence.

He edged back into the tower and reached for the railing to climb up. As he grasped it, a couple of uprights broke off and clanged down the steps.

He froze.

"Hey!"

Ware poked his head out.

The girl stood in the center of the parking area, her hands on her hips. Mirrored sunglasses flashed silver above cheeks smudged with dirt. "What are you doing here?"

Ware clambered over the rubble to the doorway. He put his hands on his hips, too. "Nothing."

"Well, this place is mine. You have to do nothing somewhere else."

"So . . ." Ware liked the word *so*. *So* bought you some time in situations like these. "So . . . you don't own this place. It's a church."

"Nuh-uh. Used to be. But now . . ." She swept her arm back over where she'd come from. "My garden."

And Ware noticed what he hadn't before: Dozens of big, squat tin cans with peeling labels, lined up among the smashed playground equipment. "A tin-can garden?"

The girl tipped her head toward the cans.

Ware walked down the steps to the parking area. He held himself tall as he passed the girl, and was relieved to see he had a couple of inches on her. Which was ridiculous—they weren't going to fight.

He crouched to study the cans. All were labeled *ChipNutz*. A knee-high plant sprouted out of each. The plants looked feathery and brave at the same time. Ware wanted to brush his fingers over their tips, but he didn't. He stood up. Beyond the cans were two rows of the same plants in the ground, chest high and sturdy.

"*My* garden," the girl called behind him. "See. This place is mine now."

It was the unfair way she claimed ownership that set Ware off. It made him want to claim something of his own. "Okay," he called over his shoulder. When he'd reached the foundation, he climbed the back steps and spread his arms over the ruins. "I'll take this."

The girl followed him to the steps. "A wrecked born-again church? Who would want that?"

"If that smashed playground is your garden, then this wrecked church is my castle." His new recklessness scared him, but he kind of liked it, too.

"Trek seven!" Kyle's voice floated over the fence.

Ware startled. He didn't have much time left.

The girl smirked. "Oh, yeah. It's a castle all right. For sinners."

"You don't know what you're talking about," he called over his shoulder, and scrambled back up onto the ruins.

eight

"Oh, I know what I'm talking about."

Unbelievable. The girl had followed him. She drew right up to him, sharp chin out, and grabbed his hand.

Ware was so stunned by the hand-grabbing that he let her pull him to the middle of the wreckage.

There, a big container clad in fake stones stood almost as tall as he was and twice as long. Ware wanted to climb those fake stones to look inside, but the girl was still holding his hand.

He didn't want her to be holding his hand, of course, but somehow he didn't feel he should take it back, either.

As a compromise, he rose on his toes to peer over the

37

top. The tub was full of wreckage, but through it, he saw that the interior was coated in glassy turquoise.

The girl dropped his hand and smacked the side of the vessel. "This here is a baptistery—a sinners' tub. People line up, begging please, oh please, could the preacher dunk them because they are suffering so from how bad they've been. Then the preacher dunks them, clothes and all, lifts them back up, and woo-hoo, they're born again, are all shiny and new, like pennies in Coke."

"Huh," Ware said. His hand was still warm from where she'd held it. It felt a little as if it might be glowing. "A magic tub."

"No. No magic tub. 'Cause the very next week, they're slinking into the Grotto, drinking the rent money, hitting their kids—same old stuff they used to do before they got dunked."

Ware sneaked a peek at his hand. It wasn't glowing, but it felt buzzy, as if it might be glowing inside. He put it into his pocket to preserve the feeling. "How do you know all this, anyway?"

"My aunt went here every Sunday till they gave up."

"Gave up?"

"Ran out of money. Quit paying, back in January. And the bank kicked them out."

"That's what happened? Why'd they knock it down?"

"Walter says so nobody could camp here, do drugs and stuff."

"Who's Walter?"

The girl hitched a shoulder toward the Grotto Bar. "Bartender."

"You know a bartender?" Ware gasped, before he could stop himself.

The girl grabbed her head and groaned.

Mortified, Ware changed the subject. "Wow. So, there must be a lot of great stuff in all this mess."

"Nuh-uh. The church people came before the wrecking crew. They took everything good."

"How do you know?"

"I watched. They took the cross out first, laid it down on a pickup truck. You notice a thing like that."

"Trek ten!"

Ware's head snapped up. He'd missed three more circuits.

The girl followed his gaze and then nodded. "You

have to go." She sounded pleased.

"I'm going." As he passed her, the oddest thing happened.

In her mirrored glasses, Ware saw himself reflected. Looking back was the most pathetic kid in the world. *You know a bartender?* Unbelievable.

nine

His mom's car and his dad's truck were parked in the driveway.

Good. He would tell them both at once, get it over with. *Chin up, chest out, advance boldly.* "I tried it. It was terrible. I'm not going back," he practiced out loud on the front step.

A lizard jumped onto the last sun-warmed patch of cement beside him and began pumping its jerky little push-ups as if cheering his proclamation. Ware didn't particularly like lizards, with their suction-cup feet, but you had to admire them, thermodynamically at least. A lizard craved the sun, but it didn't need it. It ran just fine on hot or cold blood.

41

"I mean it. I'm not going back," he repeated for the lizard. He unlocked the door.

A hushed murmuring leaked down the hall from his parents' closed bedroom door.

Closed-door was their parenting style. He hadn't minded when he was little, but now, more and more, he wished his parents would just straight-out tell him whatever was going on.

He walked down the hall and raised his knuckles to knock. Looking at his fist, he remembered: the garden-girl had held his hand.

No, that wasn't accurate. She'd only *taken* his hand, not *held* it, and she'd seemed pretty mad at him the whole time. If he'd been wearing a leash around his neck, she'd probably have dragged him over by that.

He turned his attention back to the door.

And heard: ". . . one kid. And he turns out so anti-social. He offered to pay not to go!"

Ware dropped his hand. He leaned in.

". . . now, with my mother sick. Why can't we have a normal kid?"

Ware reared back. His face flamed, but the thing in

42

his chest that felt like his soul shrank down cold, like the heart of a lizard deprived of its sun. He edged down the hall. In the kitchen, he sat at the counter and opened a game on the computer. The way a normal kid would do.

Finally, his parents emerged.

"What happened to your knee?" his father asked, his brows tented in worry.

"Nothing—it's fine." Ware stood. He cleared his throat.

"Was that a cough?" his father asked.

"No. Now, Rec."

His mother opened a drawer and started rooting around. She retrieved a lozenge, extra-strength honey lemon, and began to unwrap it.

"I'm eleven and a half, Mom." Ware groaned and pushed away the lozenge. He cleared his throat again. "So, Rec. I tried it. It was . . ."

His mother bit her bottom lip.

The sight of her anxiety hurt so much, he had to look away. "It was . . ."

He heard his mother gulp. The gulp undid him.

The terrible weight of it. The awful responsibility.

"It was . . . all right," he said, his voice quavering only slightly. He looked up.

"See?" His mother sighed, her face relaxing.

His father smiled. "You just needed to give it a chance."

And the thing in his chest uncurled just a little bit.

ten

Next day, Ware waved to his mother from the drop-off space and took a couple of normal-kid steps toward the door. When she'd driven off, he stopped. Ms. Sanchez had said he could come in whenever he wanted, and he didn't want to just yet.

He walked casually over to the oak, waited until no one was around, then tucked his backpack into the crotch of a branch and swung himself up. Just to see.

The girl sat cross-legged in the shade of three queen palms, surrounded by ChipNutz cans. It looked as if she was telling her plants a story. The palms looked like skinny old ladies in green hats, leaning down to hear the story, too, as if it was a good one.

Ware glanced over toward the church. At the top of

the baptistery, a slice of turquoise flashed like a greeting.

Lying in bed, trying to forget what he'd overheard his mother say, he'd thought about that do-over tub a lot. He could really use a brand-new-self fresh start like that.

He dropped to the ground, strode over to the girl, stood in front of her. "How does it work? Getting born again?"

"I told you. Dunking." She stabbed her trowel down next to his sneaker, a warning.

Ware took a step back. "I mean . . . the people. They weren't trying to turn into babies again, so how is it supposed to work for them?"

The girl blew her bangs out of her eyes. "They get reborn on the inside, not the outside."

For the second time in as many days, Ware remembered the laughing counselor. *No, I mean inside the group. You're outside.*

He shook it off. The outside was part of the inside.

"Right. Is everything changed, or just the bad stuff?"

"Just the bad."

"And people liked them better afterward, right?"

"Of course," the girl said. But she didn't sound quite as sure.

"Is the tub magic, or the water?"

"The water. Except it wasn't, remember? I told you it didn't work. People went right back to their old selves."

"Everybody? Nobody stayed shiny and new?"

The girl balanced her trowel on one sharp knee. She sat perfectly still except that her toes stretched in her pink flip-flops, as if they were reaching for the answer to his question. "I don't know," she admitted. "I guess I only know about one person that didn't stay born again."

"So it could work," Ware pressed. "It must work for some people, or else it wouldn't be a thing."

"Maybe." She picked up her trowel.

"Wait. The magic holy water. Was it holy to begin with, or did it get holy by being in the tub?"

"It has a regular faucet. I guess the preacher did something to it."

"What? What did they do?"

The girl blew her lips out so hard her bangs flew straight up. "Who cares? It's over! Whatever it was got packed up and left. Look around," she ordered. "There's no holy here. No magic."

Ware looked. Everything, everywhere, was broken.

Then his gaze fell upon the garden. On the plants in their rusted tin cans—feathery but brave at the same

47

time. At the bigger plants, sturdy in their row.

The girl saw where he was looking. "Nuh-uh. They're better than magic. You can count on them." She lifted her sunglasses and squinted at him. "Why are you so interested, anyway? I thought you said this was a castle. In case you didn't know it, castles don't have baptisteries."

"So . . . right. I know." Ware drew back. He suddenly felt protective about his do-over wish. As if it was feathery and brave at the same time. "But, um, ha-ha, they have moats," he joked. He added a shrug to show that he didn't really care, anyway.

"Well, far as I know, moats go *outside* a castle, not *inside*," she muttered.

And for the third time, Ware thought of that laughing counselor. He left the girl grumbling beside her plants, climbed the foundation, and headed to the do-over tub.

eleven

W are climbed the steps he'd found at the back of the baptistery and sat on the rim. He imagined the tub full of water, imagined falling into it and then stepping out a less disappointing son whose report cards said, *Ware is extremely social! And also, very normal!*

What would a change like that feel like? Would it hurt to feel your old self being kicked out? What if his old self put up a fight, or refused to budge?

At a smack on the side of the tub, he opened his eyes.

The girl again. Unbelievable. She swept off her shades and glared up.

Ware was reminded of his report. Castle battlements were slotted with narrow openings called arrow slits, through which guards could shoot approaching enemies

49

without being targets themselves. Ware got the impression that the girl's blue eyes functioned pretty much the same way.

She narrowed her arrow-slit eyes, but she was wearing a sly half smile. "How would you fill this thing?"

He gestured to the faucet.

"Nuh-uh. The city shut it off. So how would you get the water here?"

Ware looked over at the Rec Center and shuddered. Maybe the library would lend him some. "Oh, buckets," he tried in a casual tone. He tossed out a window screen.

"Nope. Hose, that's how. You got one?"

"Do I . . . ?"

"I got a hose. Fifty feet." She waved her sunglasses back toward the Grotto Bar.

"You live *in a bar*?"

"Above it. Fifty feet's not enough. It just reaches to the fence. You got a hose or not?"

"I don't know. Maybe."

"*Maybe?* Well, you bring me enough hose to reach my garden and this tub, *maybe* I won't throw you out of here." She put on her glasses and settled them firmly on her nose.

"Maybe you won't throw me . . . ?" Ware carefully straightened up to standing on the baptistery's rim. Height was an advantage in medieval warfare. "Who do you think you are, anyway?" his reckless self challenged.

The girl pursed her lips and tapped them with a grubby finger, pretending to think hard about whether to divulge this extremely important information. Then she shrugged. "Jolene."

The baptistery's rim was narrower than he'd realized. He came down a couple of steps. "Okay."

"Okay, what?"

"Okay, maybe I'll bring a hose tomorrow."

He walked past her and scooped up his backpack.

The girl followed him and jumped off the wooden-door drawbridge when he did. "Hey," she yelled as he took off for the big oak. "What's your name?"

Ware called it back to her and kept walking.

"Where? Here. What's your name *here*?"

Ware was used to this. On their first date, his parents had discovered they each had a great-great-great grand-father who'd fought at the Battle of Ware Bottom Church in the Civil War—on opposite sides. It hurt his head to think about his ancestors shooting at each other, having

no idea they'd share a great-great-great-great grandson—
what if one of them had been a better aim?—but mostly
he was glad his parents hadn't decided to commemorate
the coincidence by naming their kid Bottom.

He took a few steps back. "Not *where*," he explained,
whooshing the *h*. "Ware. With an A."

"Okay, Ware. Bring that hose. It doesn't mean you
can have the church, though. I haven't decided." She
pulled her hat out of a pocket and tugged it on.

Ware felt his jaw drop at the unfairness. He really
hated unfairness. He wanted to say something stinging
back at her, but before she'd tugged her hat down, her
mirror glasses had pulled that trick again. And there he
was, still the most pathetic kid in the world. He hadn't
even thought about how he'd fill that do-over tub.

He started toward the Rec again, head down. "Wait,"
he heard. He waited.

"What's 'Ix'?"

He turned.

The girl was pointing up to the wall by the doorway.
"Ix," she repeated. "What's it mean?"

"Not Ix. Nine. In Roman numerals."

"Why?"

He walked back. "They used Roman numerals back in the Middle Ages. And they put sundials on castle walls. See how the shadow is pointing toward the numerals? I made them at nine o'clock yesterday."

"Oh. So, here"—she tapped the wall—"this is ten o'clock?"

"Around there. But I'd have to be here at ten to make sure."

She cocked her head at the numerals. "Is that *blood*?"

Ware nodded miserably.

"Huh," she said, frowning. She seemed to be trying hard to decide something—for real this time.

Ware took the opportunity to escape. He was nearly to the fence when she ran over to him.

"The parking lot is the boundary. Between my territory and yours. No crossing it. And you can't tell anyone about this place."

"What?"

"I decided. You can have the church."

twelve

The next morning after his mother drove away, Ware jumped up into the oak and concealed himself in a cloud of leaves, deep as a secret, because the first objective of medieval reconnaissance was to gather information about the enemy.

And in spite of the hand taking with the buzzy feeling, in spite of allowing him the church, that's what the garden girl was. She'd made that clear. What she didn't know was that Ware was an expert in castle defense. He'd gotten an A on his report.

The enemy was digging in the shade of the three queen palms. The palms looked like guards today, curving over Jolene protectively.

Ware noted how carefully she placed her foot on the

spade before jumping on it, probably so it wouldn't cut through her flip-flops. The enemy's inadequate footgear was a clear weakness.

Her trowel jutted out of a back pocket. Obviously gardening was a strength, but strengths, he reminded himself, could be useful as diversionary tactics.

He released his backpack, heavy with a hose he'd found in his shed, and dropped down after it.

Jolene turned at the thud. "The boundary," she yelled, waving a finger at the parking area.

Ware hoisted the hose like a white flag.

Jolene nodded permission and he crossed, dropped it in front of her. "What are you doing?"

She joggled her free hand through the air, as though hunting for the words to adequately express how deranged his question was.

"I mean, I see what you're doing. But why?"

Jolene kicked at a pile of dirt. "It's basically rock dust. I have to dig out a trench and fill it with good soil before I can put in my plants."

Ware took a step closer. "I mean, why are you doing all this work? What's so important about these plants?"

Jolene jumped on her shovel again, this time not so

carefully. Her hair flopped down like a curtain, but not before Ware had seen her face. She looked frightened.

His hand flew to his chest, the way it always did. The sight of people being frightened literally stole his breath, like a hundred-arrow volley to the lungs, *thunk-thunk-thunk*.

Mikayla was always stunned at how deeply Ware sensed other people's pain. "It's like your superpower," she said, "feeling what other people are feeling."

"Right. Captain Empathy," Ware had joked back. But he hadn't really thought it was funny. Superpowers weren't supposed to hurt.

Now he wanted to tell Jolene not to be afraid. But nowhere in his research for his report had he learned that a good castle defense was to tell the enemy not to be afraid.

He backed away and climbed onto the foundation to accomplish the second objective of reconnaissance: location assessment. Location assessment required height, so he picked his way over to the tower. Towers were excellent for getting the whole picture of a place.

The stairway, he noted as he climbed, spiraled the wrong way, at least for real medieval castles. Real castle stairways wound up counter-clockwise so that the castle defenders, streaming down from the top, would have their right arms free to do battle with the ascending attackers, who would have their sword arms to the wall.

But Ware was left-handed. The clockwise spiral felt like a sign. This place was meant for him.

Which was crazy, of course.

From the top of the tower—which wasn't exactly towering, maybe twenty feet high—he did get the whole picture of the place.

The lot was almost as big as a football field, and protected from view all the way around, the way castles were protected by their outer curtain walls. The side boundaries—east and west—were six-foot board fences, while the north boundary in the back had even taller evergreen hedges. All of First Street was marked *Glory Alliance Parking Only!* and the bank had erected a tall chain-link fence covered in orange mesh and warning signs across the front lawn. The same construction fencing had gone up across the driveway in the back that led to the small parking area. Even the nosiest person pressing an eye to that fencing would have a hard time seeing what went on in the lot.

Ware looked down at Jolene. She was dabbing her trowel over each plant down the row, like a fairy godmother bestowing blessings with her wand. And then he realized: She wasn't blessing her plants, she was counting them. As if they could have grown legs and escaped during the night.

When she picked up the hose and began to water them, it dawned on him: If he wanted to try out that do-over tub—and he did, although he'd have to keep it secret from her, of course—he had the upper hand now, thanks to that hose. She'd have to tell him whatever she knew about the holy water deal.

He hurried down the tower stairs, jumped off the back of the foundation. Chin up, chest out, he advanced boldly into her territory.

thirteen

"This good soil you need," Ware said, employing Jolene's strength as a diversionary tactic before sneaking into the holy water issue. "Where are you going to get it?"

Jolene nodded approvingly at the question. She twisted the hose nozzle off and waved toward three waist-high heaps he hadn't noticed before.

The piles were layered with food in various stages of rot. Banana peels, orange and watermelon rinds, some greenish stuff that must have once been vegetables. "Garbage?"

"It was," she agreed. "It's turning into compost."

Ware hitched his eyebrows into a look that he hoped conveyed sufficient wonder. "Compost. Great. Now, what did the preacher do to make the water holy?"

She tipped her head to the fence behind the piles. "I go to the Greek Market next door and get the fruits and vegetables too old to sell. I shovel some dirt over them and the worms do the rest. Now, the Chinese were the first to compost, back in 2000 BC, and . . ."

Ware started to zone out, but when the sun pulled out of the queen palm fronds and hit her mirror glasses, it jolted him.

At his grandmother's place, Ware had gotten up at dawn to have the pool to himself. That early, the water would flash blindingly, like those glasses. No matter how hard he'd tried to peer down into it, he'd only seen his own face reflected back. Sometimes, yourself was exactly what you didn't want to see.

"Oh," he said, a little unnerved for a moment. "So . . . the preacher. Was it a spell?"

"Look. I only snuck in once. I heard some words that sounded important." Jolene pushed her hat up and studied his head for a thoughtful moment. "You look like you're rusting."

Ware rubbed his hair. He knew it was unusual— his mom's tight waves, his dad's dark copper color. But the summer sun bleached it bronze, and three weeks of chlorine at Sunset Palms hadn't helped. "I know," he said. "But what about—"

Jolene flapped her trowel at him dismissively. "No offense. My freckles look greenish in the sun. Now, there are three piles because they're in different stages—"

They both turned at the shriek of a whistle.

The Rec kids were outside. They began to cheer.

"Rec–re–ation
 On va–cation
 We're fun–nation
 Go, Rec, GO!"

Several times a day the campers were gathered in a circle to link arms for something called Rec Spirit. Ware hadn't liked the shouting, and he'd never understood the cheer.

At home after his first day, he'd asked his mother what recreation meant.

"Play. You know, things you do for fun. Not work."

None of those definitions applied to the day he'd just had. "How about funnation? What does that mean?"

"It's not a word," she'd said. "You must have heard it wrong."

He'd listened carefully the next day, and when he heard the word again, he'd unhooked an elbow and raised his hand. "Is it Fun Nation? Or fun-ation?" The counselor had just stared at him. "It's *funnation*," she'd said unhelpfully. "So it *rhymes*."

From then, he'd shouted the cheer along with everyone else, but it always left him feeling vaguely embarrassed.

"Hey, wake up." Jolene waggled her fingers toward the Rec. "You have to go. Bye."

"Not yet." Ware heard the words as if it had come from someone else. "First, I have something important to do."

fourteen

Ware shoved the big wooden door over the side until it thudded to the ground. If he was going to have a castle, its drawbridge was going to welcome him.

Then, trip after trip, he hauled junk out of the baptistery and into the dumpsters at the back of the property. At the bottom, he discovered a problem: a massive brass bell. The wrecking ball must have knocked it out of the tower.

He needed some rope to haul out that bell. Somewhere in this mess there must be some rope.

He began the search in what used to be the kitchen. A long butcher-block table stood stolidly bearing its load of rubble, but most everything else had been crushed. He yanked open the few cupboards that were still accessible.

Plastic and paper supplies; burned pans and cracked dishes; a bottle of grape juice, furred with mold. Jolene was right: all the good stuff had been scooped.

Next to the kitchen had been a dining hall. It had probably held a flock of tables and chairs, but now only the collapsed roof furnished the space. At the far end, though, stood three closets, barely touched.

Ware clambered over the wreckage and cleared enough space to open the doors. The first was a janitor's closet—cleaning supplies, mops, buckets, and brooms.

The shelves of the next closet were empty except for some red-and-white-checkered vinyl tablecloths and a wooden box full of candle stubs with a lighter on top. More junk, no rope.

The last closet was full of art supplies—cases of glue, cartons of markers and crayons, jars of glitter and finger paint, a pile of Noah's ark coloring books.

He flipped through the top one and a memory surfaced.

The first summer, after a trip to the zoo, the Rec kids had been marched into the Art Hut to draw an animal they'd seen.

"What's this?" the counselor had asked, holding up

Ware's drawing—dramatic blazes of black and orange spiraling into a joyful scribble of green.

"The tiger." Ware had been so proud, he'd raised his voice so all the kids could hear—this would make up for the inside/outside thing. "It's escaping. Remember, its face was sad?"

"Well, that's okay," the counselor had said, "not everyone can be an artist." She'd moved away, pinning up the drawings the other kids had done by tracing lions and elephants and bears. Ware had crumpled his drawing and stuffed it in the trash.

He shook off the memory. He was about to leave when he spied a fresh pack of Play-Doh at the back.

He split the cellophane and peeled up the lids. The weird chemical vanilla smell made his fingers ache to plunge into the smooth mounds, but he thought about Sad Girl and snapped the lids back on. Clay was only perfect once.

The room at the corner must have been an office. Wooden bookshelves collapsed against the broken walls, their shelves bare except for a bag of black plastic letters and numbers and a cardboard box.

The box was damp and smelled defeated, like mold.

He opened the lid and lifted out a framed photograph: a brown-toned picture of the church, its roof only a skeleton of beams, surrounded by men raising hammers and saws. The year *1951* was written in faded ink on the back.

He flipped through other pictures. Weddings and funerals; young men in soldiers' uniforms; beaming women holding pies in gloved hands; children in bathrobes adoring baby dolls in mangers.

The pictures reminded Ware of the tapestries that royal ladies wove for their castles. Those tapestries kept out the winter drafts, but their true purpose was much more important. People passing by learned the stories of the castle from the panels hanging outside—births and deaths, battles and unions, acts of heroism or mystic encounters.

These pictures weren't so different from those tapestries, he realized. They weren't different at all.

He held up another. In it, a stained-glass window was being installed in the west wall.

He carried the photo to the spot and tossed away junk until he found the remains: a thousand shards of colored glass glittering through the debris. He picked some out and cradled them in his palm—ruby, sapphire, emerald, and amber. They shone like doomed jewels.

He propped up the photograph to tell its story— *Once, a window glowed here*—and made his way back.

He re-covered the box and pushed it deeper under the shelf so rain wouldn't ruin it. A folder that had been underneath fell to the floor.

Ware picked it up. The question on its cover—ARE YOU LEADING A PURPOSE-DRIVEN LIFE?—electrified him as if a switch had been thrown.

What *was* a purpose-driven life? What purpose could drive *his*? These seemed like exactly the kinds of things a person trying to get himself reborn should ask.

He flipped open the cover in tremendous excitement.

The folder was empty.

Ware slumped against the bookcase.

Are you leading a purpose-driven life?

What a question.

fifteen

Ware found his parents splayed across the living room couch as if they'd been blown there by cannon, too exhausted to even look shocked about it. The pregame was on with no sound—his dad believed announcers ruined baseball—and a pizza box sat on the coffee table.

His mother shook her head as if to clear it. "Hey, there. You have a good day?"

Guilt over ditching Rec coated Ware like grime. He'd meant to go. He'd actually made it to the door and reached for the bar handle. But inside, they were shouting again. His soul had retreated and his arm had fallen back to his side. Whatever funnation was, he wasn't. He'd placed the Play-Doh on the step and bolted back to the lot.

Jolene had vanished, so Ware climbed the tower and ate his lunch surveying his kingdom.

His kingdom, he'd seen from there, was a mess.

So he'd come down, gotten a push broom, and started clearing the floor around the baptistery. When a blister on his palm made that too painful, he located a window screen and some glue and set them on the kitchen work table. He gathered all the broken pieces of stained glass big enough to salvage and began sticking them to the screen— an explosion of smashed gems, come to life again.

He'd had a *great* day.

Now he considered the possible answers to his mother's question. His parents had been working double shifts for nearly a month. They might be too tired to care if he admitted he hadn't gone to Rec. "I had a *really* good day," he began cautiously.

Before he could go on, his mother sighed with dramatic relief. "Oh, thank goodness. We're so glad you're making it work."

Ware winced. "Dad . . ."

"We both appreciate it, son." He pointed at the TV screen, where players were running around the bases. "Think of it like that. A sacrifice fly. Not great for the player, but best for the team. There's no 'I' in team, you know."

"Or think of it as your job this summer," his mother chimed in. "To help us buy this house."

"My job is going to Rec?"

"No, your job is making sure we don't worry about you. And don't forget, we owe you something nice at the end. Do you know what you want?"

Ware shook his head. He just wanted summer to be over.

"Now, what is it you did today that was so much fun?"

"So . . ." He turned to the television. "Just, you know, normal stuff." He pushed the word *normal* a little extra, then risked a glance to see how it had gone over.

His mother smiled and pushed the pizza box toward him along with a stack of napkins.

Ware sat on the rug and took a slice, although he'd just lost his appetite.

Just then, his mother's phone rang. "Your grand-mother's hospital," she announced. She left to take the call in the bedroom, closed-door style.

When she came back, she was trailing a suitcase.

"Eight tomorrow morning for the surgery. I'll go down tonight, after work. I'll stay until she can be moved."

Ware put down his slice. "Is she scared?"

"What? No." His mother looked puzzled. "I mean, maybe. I don't know."

"Tell her I'll come see her. Can I?"

"It's 'may,' not 'can.' And yes. She'll be at a rehab place nearby." She shouldered her pocketbook. "I almost forgot. Uncle Cy is coming. He'll stay with us a few days."

"Oh, good." Ware's uncle wasn't like other grown-ups. When Uncle Cy asked you a question, he actually listened to the answer. But he worked for a news organization, filming documentaries all over the world, and the few times he came to the States, it was usually to Los Angeles or New York.

His mom studied him, hand on a hip. "I don't know what it is, but you remind me of him at your age." She grabbed her suitcase, kissed the top of his head, and pointed to the kitchen. "I left you a schedule."

Ware sighed. Of course she did.

sixteen

The schedule was three pages long.

Ware sighed again. Beside him, his father sighed, too. His father's sigh was admiring and Ware's was despairing, but both were heartfelt.

"She needed to tell me when to put on sunscreen?"

His father leaned in for a closer look. "Every four hours," he confirmed. "And look. She's labeled the tubes. One for each week."

None of it surprised Ware. His mother was a walking daily planner. She had an infallible internal clock and a memory that archived every appointment time for eternity.

Once, while shopping, she'd passed a big digital

display that read 2:55. "Oh," she said wistfully, "two fifty-five! First Monday of every month, I'd leave the office at two fifty-five. Pick you up from school at seven past three, have you at your orthodontist at three twenty-five. We'd sit in the car for exactly four minutes while you complained about having braces and then we'd walk in right on time. Remember?"

His braces had come off six months ago. He remembered the fruity cleaning-supplies smell of the office, the way the orthodontist's hairs had sprouted out of his nose, and how sharply the braces bit each time they were tightened. But no, he did not remember the time.

"Think of it this way," his father interrupted Ware's thoughts. "It's fourth down, fourth quarter, a minute to go and we're behind. The quarterback, your mother, calls for a *Red Right Thirty Pull Trap*. The touchdown depends on every player being exactly where he's supposed to be, doing exactly what he's supposed to do exactly when he's supposed to do it. You get it?"

Ware nodded vigorously, as if he *totally* got it. He stared hard at the schedule, pretending to ponder the advice deeply.

Moments like this, he always felt lonely, as if sports were a planet his father lived on, a planet he could never travel to.

Worse, Ware knew his dad felt lonely at these times, too. Sometimes he would look at his son with a baffled expression, the kind of expression someone getting ready to dig into a big steak might wear when he realized there were only a couple of cotton balls next to the plate instead of a knife and a fork. *What am I supposed to do with this?* the expression asked.

Ware didn't want to see that expression right now, so he nodded some more.

Beside him, Ware's dad stretched out his arm. He eyed his watch, then took it off.

"What are you doing?" Ware asked, shocked. Unlike his mother, his father didn't have an infallible internal clock, and he worried about forgetting some important appointment, such as watching a ball game. To prevent this tragedy, he wore a wristwatch able to maintain several alarms at once.

His father clasped the watch around Ware's wrist.

"But you need this, Dad."

74

"Not as much as you do," he said with another deep sigh. Then he headed back to the couch.

Ware put the schedule back on the fridge next to the Rec brochure. The only appointment he didn't want to miss was with the three forty-five bus home. He set the watch for three thirty, then chose a birdcall for the alarm.

Birds symbolized freedom. Which he would never have.

seventeen

Ware smiled at the sight of his hose curled beside Jolene like a faithful dog. Today, he'd haul out the bell with the rope he'd found in his shed, then fill the baptistery and get himself born again. A penny in Coke.

He dropped from the branch and ran over to Jolene.

"Nuh-uh. Boundaries."

"We don't need boundaries," Ware said. He had thought about this all night. People defending castles needed to work together. That's why they held games and festivals—to practice their cooperation, enhance their loyalty. "The lot is ours, together. We're on the same team."

Jolene sat back on her heels, a wary look on her face.

"Think of it like football," he tried. "A pull trap. Red. For the touchdown."

Jolene just stared.

"Never mind." He sighed. He pointed to the hose. "It's my turn."

"Your turn?"

"With the hose. Remember?"

Jolene dropped her trowel and trekked over to the Grotto Bar–side fence. Her left flip-flop flashed the dull silver of duct tape with every step. She bent to the hose coupling. It looked as if she was disconnecting her hose from his.

She *was* disconnecting hers from his.

She walked back and pointed to his hose. "Okay. You can take it now."

"What do you mean? It's not going to work now. It's got no water!"

Jolene looked back to the separated ends. "Correct. No water now."

"But the deal. Remember? I bring a hose, we hook it up to yours, and we both get to use them."

Jolene tapped a grubby finger to her lip and scrunched her face. "Nuh-uh, that wasn't the deal," she said after a thoughtful moment. "The deal was: you bring me your hose, I wouldn't kick you out of here. Which I didn't."

"That's not fair!" Ware really, really hated unfairness.

Jolene's jaw fell open. A happily startled expression lit her face. "Wha . . . ?" she gasped, looking around the lot. "Is this Magic Fairness Land???" Then her shoulders drooped. "Nope, darn. Still here in the real world." She picked up her trowel.

Ware felt his jaw clench again. "So, you . . . you're seriously going to cheat me?"

Jolene clapped a hand to her chest, as though deeply wounded. "Of course not. We're going to make a new deal is all. You dig me some new trench today, I'll let you use my hose."

She pointed to a spade leaning against the fence and smiled brightly.

Ware lifted his chin and thrust out his chest, as if he was not quite the most pathetic kid in the world. "Fine," he conceded boldly. "But the new deal is also this: no more boundaries."

eighteen

"The Greeks were *on* it," Jolene said, speaking in the kind of awed tone people usually reserved for superheroes. "In 500 BC they ruled that garbage had to be buried at least a mile from the city."

Ware's palms burned and his shoulders ached. Sweat rolled in currents down his back. He gritted his teeth as the lecture dragged on.

"In Britain, everybody was croaking left and right from the Black Plague because the streets were piled with garbage and rats and all. So they invented a job where men called rakers raked the trash off the streets."

Ware had to admit that part was kind of interesting. The Black Plague hadn't killed as many people in castles as in cities, because castles had cats and dogs to keep the rats out of the grain stores. Still, he wished he could go back in time and tell those knights, *Thou shalt pick up the trash*.

"The ancient Romans used their urine for lots of things," Jolene went on. "Growing juicier pomegranates, whitening their teeth, cleaning their clothes."

"Castle defenders threw pots of it at invaders trying to climb over the walls," Ware countered. "It was a weapon. Urine!"

Jolene nodded approvingly. "Repurposing." Then she moved on to papayas. "Two hundred thirty-six seeds I got out of that single rotten papaya she gave me," she marveled.

Ware figured he should act as if he was listening until he got his hands on the hose, so he asked, "Who?"

"Mrs. Stavros. She owns the Greek Market. I told you: she gives me stuff for my compost." She raised a palm to the seedlings. "I only have forty-seven cans, so that's all the seeds I could plant this time. I could have had two hundred thirty-six plants right now if I'd had enough cans."

"Too bad," Ware said, secretly relieved there'd been only forty-seven. He wiped at the sweat pouring down his face. "You sure must love papayas."

"Oh, I love them, all right. A papaya will give you fruit in just ten months. These first ones will start ripening in October. Like, fifty on a plant! A hundred plants could give you five thousand fruits. If each of those had two hundred thirty-six seeds . . . Anyway, the point is, we need to do a lot more digging."

Jolene stabbed her shovel into the hard dirt and threw a load over her shoulder.

A clod hit Ware in the ear and clumped onto his sweaty neck. He brushed it off and was weighing the odds Jolene would let him wash up with her hose when he heard a rustling.

He leaned away from Jolene's furious digging and listened.

Someone was inside the lot.

nineteen

An older girl, fourteen at least, emerged from the bushes at the corner of the foundation and marched down the handicapped ramp. Her shorts were knife crisp and so white they hurt Ware's eyes.

At the bottom, the girl scanned the parking area and frowned. She began taking careful leaping steps along its curb, like a gymnast on a beam. She held her arms out, pointer fingers extended as if warning the world not to mess with her balance. A neat ponytail flicked up behind her at each leap. Ware liked the look of that ponytail, slick and black and acting all surprised.

Without taking his eyes off the intruder, he tapped Jolene's back.

"What—"

"Shhh."

Jolene straightened. For a moment, she watched with her mouth agape, as if she couldn't believe what her eyes were telling her. "Hey!" she yelled.

The girl brushed a cool glance over them, then began leaping again. She stopped at the corner, pulled out a phone, and took a picture of the asphalt. Then she began pacing the curb with the same gymnast steps.

Jolene came to life. Her hat flew off as she charged, legs pumping like pistons, still wielding the trowel. "Hey. This is our place!"

Ware dropped his shovel. He hated fights, fights made his soul retreat to a tiny kernel, but he hurried after her. Jolene had just called the lot *their place. Theirs*, together. Just like that. It was a thrilling development.

Drawing up, Ware could see the girl was even older than he'd thought. Fifteen at least. He dragged his fingers through his hair, sticky with sweat, and reseated his cap.

"First of all," the girl said to Jolene, "this is *not* your place. This is parcel number 788, owned by Sun Shores Bank."

Jolene leaned in. "You work for a bank? They let a kid work for a bank? I want to talk to someone there!"

The girl laughed and shook her head. "I want to talk to someone there, too. Or whoever buys this place at auction. But it's definitely not your—"

"Auction? What auction?" Jolene was glowering over the rims of her sunglasses, but just for an instant Ware had seen it again: the look of fear on her face. The look that pierced his heart, *thunk-thunk-thunk.*

The girl stepped back. "Um . . . it's foreclosed? That's what happens. Anyway—"

"When?" Jolene demanded.

The girl threw her hands up. "I don't know! Forget it. I don't work for a bank, remember?" She took out her phone again, snapped another picture over Jolene's shoulder, and tapped a few keys.

Then she turned to Ware. "Look, I'm finished now. You two can get on with your . . . um, mud fight?"

Ware ducked his face into the neck of his tee and swiped, wishing he'd gotten to the hose. He heard Jolene mutter, "Don't come back."

The girl shrugged. "I won't."

Jolene headed up to her plants as if she'd won something.

Ware wasn't so sure. He caught up with the girl at

the rear of the foundation. "Wait. You said you weren't coming back, but somebody else is, right?"

"Actually, a lot of somebodies? The bank people, whoever they get to put up security lights. I'll let the Audubon Society know—"

"No! Nobody can come here!"

At his shout, Jolene shot up and came tearing back over.

"Someone's coming here?" she sputtered. "Who?"

The girl tipped her head to the sky, as if she were deciding something. "Okay, whatever," she said after a moment. "Here's the deal."

twenty

The new girl climbed the back steps, sat primly at the top, and looked down at them like a teacher waiting for her class to settle.

Jolene planted herself at the base of the steps, arms crossed.

Ware perched on the railing. He was still feeling a little dizzy. *Their* lot.

"In low light," the girl began, "wet pavement can look like water to waterfowl. Geese, ducks, cranes."

"Who's coming here?" Jolene demanded. "And by the way, they can't."

The girl arched a single dark eyebrow and began again calmly. "Wet pavement, in low light? They think it's water, try to land on it, and they break their legs."

"Even if that's true," Jolene interrupted, "what's it got to do with our lot?"

"Um, again . . . *your* lot?" The girl rolled her eyes.

Again, *their* lot.

Jolene ignored the eye roll. "So, what? You're afraid some geese are going to crash down here?"

"Not geese." The girl pointed straight up. "This is a sandhill crane flyway. Every fall, thousands of them migrate right over this place. This *exact place*, which now, with the church moved out, is unlit. I just measured the parking lot: about ninety feet by fifty. That's a big enough patch of pavement to be a problem. Plus, see how the driveway curves into it? Like a river. If it's wet and dark when they fly over . . ."

Ware looked back at the parking lot. He couldn't help picturing it covered with crashed birds, hurt and scared.

He groaned.

"Exactly. A sandhill crane weighs ten pounds. That's a lot of bird landing on two skinny legs." She rose and brushed off her shorts, which had remained miraculously spotless. "But not on my watch."

As she passed, Ware caught the crisp scent of apple shampoo. He wished again he'd run that hose over his face.

"What are you going to do?" Jolene asked. "Send the bird police? Set up detour signs?"

"Hilarious. Sandhill cranes have been doing this for millions of years, so neither of those would even work. Those birds are *coming*. I'm making a list of all the danger spots in the city. My father's a city councilman. I'm going to have him order the owners to light them up. I'll also bring the Audubon people here, see what they can do."

Jolene shot her palms out. "Nope!"

"Nope!" Ware dropped from the railing.

The girl looked from one to the other. "Um . . . yes?" She pulled her ponytail over her shoulder and twirled the end. "My father will get it done. He's already agreed."

"Well, make him unagree then," Jolene said. "No bringing those bank people. No bringing those bird people."

The girl looked them over again. "What is it with you two? What've you got going on here?"

twenty-one

"Tell me about your day."

Ware looked up at his father, stretched out on the couch, and considered. He really did want to tell someone about his day. He'd called his friends, but Mikayla had gone up north with a friend and Vashon was at basketball camp.

He fixed his gaze on the silent ball game and began. "That empty lot beside the community center. Apparently it's on a migration flyway. Thousands of cranes fly over. Tens of thousands."

His dad settled deeper into the couch. "Mm-hmm."

"Remember I told you the church was gone? A wrecking ball did it. They took out most of the stuff, but they left anything too heavy, or bolted down. Like, the pews. You could sit on them if you cleared off the wreckage."

Ware paused, sure his dad would ask how he knew all this: Wasn't he in Rec? At best, he'd definitely warn him about trespassing or rusty nails.

But his dad remained quiet, his eyes closed as if waiting for more. Ware relaxed a little. It felt good to be listened to.

"They left the baptistery behind. I didn't know what it was, but another kid told me."

Ware paused again, thinking about "another kid." He could still feel the moment Jolene had taken his hand, how it had stayed warm. He couldn't remember another time someone had held his hand, although his parents must have when he was little. He leaned back and rested his head very softly against his father's knee. His dad didn't move.

"People get dunked in the water," he added, edging up to the important part. "And they get born again."

Ware waited. Again, his dad said nothing.

"I was thinking that might be good for me. This time, I could try to be more like you and Mom."

Ware held himself perfectly still. He had said it. Out

loud. *Oh, no. We don't want you to change a bit!* his dad might answer. Or, *That would be terrific, son!*

Ware didn't know which response he'd like better. Or which response would make him feel worse.

Just then, his dad's arm dropped off the couch and clocked him on the cheek. Ware panicked for a second— eyes closed, mouth slack, his father looked too much like the people rolling by on gurneys at the hospital the other night. But then he let out a shuddering snore and Ware breathed again.

He picked up his dad's arm and tucked it gently back on the cushion.

He nudged up the volume until he could hear the announcer. It wasn't much, but when his dad woke up, at least Ware could give him the play-by-play.

twenty-two

After a good five minutes of pulling with the rope, Ware finally heard the bell budge with a crunching groan. He ran back and peered over the edge.

The news was bad. The bell had busted a crater in the bottom of the baptistery.

The thing in his chest that must be his soul took the news hard. He collapsed onto a step.

The do-over tub would never hold water.

He would never be reborn.

For the rest of his life, he would be the same not-normal, outside-the-inside, antisocial disappointment of a son to his parents. A kid whose every report card would say *Ware needs to participate more in class!* when by "participate" they meant shout out answers without taking time to consider them. Or *Ware is very bright, but keeps this hidden!* Or, once, *Sometimes I forget Ware is in my class!*

What kind of a teacher forgets about a kid just because he's quiet?

Just then, a lizard hopped onto the step beside him and blew out its scarlet neck flap. "I'm not looking for a fight," Ware assured it, hands up.

The old church was littered with lizards, baking on the hot concrete rubble. Ware didn't begrudge them the space, but they always reminded him of the day he'd heard his mother say she wished her son was normal. It would have been better if he'd seen a different animal that day. Something less common, like the luna moth he'd found out there once trembling on the screen door: pale milky green, big as his hand.

"Go away," he told the lizard beside him now.

The lizard blinked.

Ware bent for a closer look. Lizards, like cats and camels and aardvarks, he remembered, had an extra, translucent eyelid—a nictitating membrane that they could draw across their eyes vertically like drawing the curtains, like saying, *No, thanks very much, I'm enjoying some private time right now.*

The lizard had some antisocial eyelids. Maybe it was the right animal to have seen after all. Maybe he *should* keep remembering what a disappointment he was.

His eyes pricked with tears and his throat stung. He pressed his head between his knees, glad no one was around.

After a minute, he heard the sound of metal scraping on the pavement below. He peeked over the rim of the baptistery.

Jolene was dragging a caveman hammer across the parking area. Leather gloves swamped her elbows and a pair of safety glasses hung from her neck. Her face wore the most purpose-driven expression Ware had ever seen.

He climbed out and stood in the back doorway. She was actually going to try it.

Yesterday, she'd driven the girl—Ashley, it turned out her name was—out of the lot by promising to get rid of the bird-bone-breaking pavement. "Presto: no pavement, no problem. So no bank people, no bird people, no lights, and no *you!*"

Ashley had snorted. But Jolene shot her a look of such smoking rage, she'd scrambled over the chain-link fence and hopped on her bike. "Whatever," she'd called before speeding off. "I'll come back next week, see if you've really done it."

Ware figured Jolene had been bluffing, because afterward, she'd refused to talk about it. She just checked the sun the way she had the day before, then hid her tools in the hedge, pulled out a black garbage bag, and left with it.

But now here she was. She drew a foot-long spike from her belt, crouched, and worked it into a crack in the pavement. Then she stood up, snapped on the glasses, hoisted the hammer, and slammed it down with a ringing smash.

Jolene looked up at him and pointed down.

Ware shook his head. Her crazy promise was her crazy promise.

She continued pointing.

He walked down the stairs and ambled over. Just to see.

A wedge of asphalt had split off.

"Haul it away."

Ware looked up toward the useless baptistery. His throat tightened again. "No. I don't care who comes. I'm done here. Sorry, Jolene." He started to walk toward the

Rec. His legs felt like stone.

"Well, sorry yourself, Ware. You're still helping move this pavement."

Ware kept walking. "No, I'm not. Goodbye, Jolene."

"Yeah-huh, you are. Because . . ."

There was a pause. Then he heard, "I need you." The quaver in Jolene's voice rang like an alarm.

He turned and the arrow volley struck him: *thunk-thunk-thunk*, all one hundred arrows landing true. He ran back, hand to his chest.

Jolene blinked back her tears, stood up straighter. "Mrs. Stavros at the Greek Market will sell whatever I grow." She sniffed. "It's a lot of bunny. Which I need."

"A lot of bunny?"

Jolene sniffed again. "Money. I said money."

"Oh. But . . . but you can't do it, Jolene. You just can't chop up a parking lot and carry it away."

"Well, I have to. Otherwise that rich girl is going to bring all those nosy people here and I'm going to lose this place." She lost her fight with the tears. They spilled down her cheeks. "I can't lose this place."

Those tears.

"Okay, okay, wait," he said. "Let me think."

He looked around, as if an answer might be floating in the air, and saw the watchtower. Watchtowers were excellent for getting the whole picture. For seeing things clearly.

"Stay here," he said. "Don't be afraid." Then he climbed.

From the top, he got the whole picture all right. He saw things clearly.

And his heart lifted. It actually lifted, just like in books, and hope flooded into the space created.

The bird-bone-breaking pavement—walkways front and sides, and the back parking lot—circled the church like a moat.

Like a *moat*.

twenty-three

Ware pointed to the inner corner of the parking area, where a couple of inches of water had pooled. "That's from last night's rain. The drain is clogged with building junk. We'll clog up the other drains, too."

"What about, you know, gravity?" Jolene blurted beside him, wiping her cheeks.

"Gravity?"

Jolene waved her arms over the outer sides of the parking area. "What's going to hold the water in over there? And all around?" Her arms kept up the waving, almost hysterically.

Ware waved his own arms toward the foundation. "There must be a million concrete blocks up there. We'll build a wall. All the way around. We're making a moat."

Jolene's arms dropped as though they were too stunned to hold themselves up. "Could we really do that?"

Ware imagined it. Water stretching into an immense pool, three feet deep at the back, guarding his castle. *You see that? Wow.*

The queen palms seemed to be nodding encouragement, as if hoping to see themselves reflected in the water's surface.

Two kids build a moat, Ware voice-overed in his head. *Can they do it?*

"Okay, yeah, I guess we have to," Jolene said.

Ware froze. Had he spoken it aloud?

And then an even more shocking thought struck him. It wasn't just a bird-protecting moat they'd be making.

It was a giant get-born-again, penny-in-Coke, do-over tub.

Holy water—whatever it was—he was sure going to need a lot of it.

twenty-four

The problem was that the wrecking ball hadn't knocked the walls down into nice clean individual concrete blocks. Ware lugged out maybe a dozen singles before running out. There were a few two- and three-block chunks, but the rest were mortared together in big slabs, some the size of cars, with twisted metal rods spiking out of them.

Ware bent to a five-block hunk and pulled with everything he had. The hunk did not budge. It seemed to be smirking. "Can we crack it apart up here?"

"Better not," Jolene decided. "That front opening is pretty big. We can't let anyone see. Down in the parking lot."

Ware retrieved his rope and tied it around the hunk.

After five minutes of pulling together, they managed to drag it to the back doorway. After another mighty tug, it smashed down into the parking area.

Ware followed, staggered to a patch of grass, and collapsed. He wished he'd played a sport, any sport, and grown some muscles.

Jolene snapped her safety glasses down and wedged her spike into a crack in the center. When it was upright, she hoisted the sledgehammer. For a moment it waggled above her head on her spaghetti arms. But then she got control and the hammer smashed down true. The chunk split in half.

"You look . . . ," Ware began, then searched for a word up to the task. "Heroic" came up and that word was right, but his shocked mouth refused to utter it.

"I know what I look like," Jolene grumbled. She stretched the glasses off her face and scowled at them, then let them snap onto the top of her head. "But Mrs. Stavros says if I don't wear them, she'll take back her tools. Plus she says I'll never get another rotten banana from her."

"What? Who?" Ware asked, still dazed that he'd nearly called this grubby girl heroic.

"Mrs. Stavros, remember? The lady that gives me all the rotten fruit."

Ware corrected her absently, "Who."

"Mrs. Stavros. I already *told* you about her."

"No, I mean it's 'who,' not 'that.'"

The instant he said the words, he regretted them—it irritated him when his mother corrected his grammar. But Jolene was staring at him for an explanation, and there was no exit sign in that stare.

"'Who' is for people and 'that' is for things. So it's 'Mrs. Stavros is the lady *who*,' not 'the lady *that*.'"

Jolene dropped her hammer and fell back on her butt.

"Sorry," Ware said. "It doesn't matter." He walked over to the broken chunk of wall and grabbed hold of the smaller piece—a double block. He risked a glance at her, still on the ground.

Her knuckles whitened around the spike. "No one ever told me that rule."

"For real, it doesn't matter. Lots of people make that mistake." Ware locked his knees and hoisted the chunk to his shins. Before he could attempt a step, his legs started shaking. He dropped the chunk and wiped his brow.

"It's a *good* rule." Jolene fumed as if he hadn't spoken,

as if he weren't even there. "Because people aren't things. You can throw things away. Usually you shouldn't. But sometimes, things are trash. But people are never trash. So it's good that people get a different word. I am a person *who* knows that."

twenty-five

Jolene shot the hose stream straight up in a spray that spattered the queen palms' fronds. The palms fluttered delightedly in the reverse rain and dripped over Ware and Jolene lying underneath.

While they cooled off, Ware made some calculations. "We built five feet of wall this morning, and it's in the back, where it needs to be tallest. The perimeter is around four hundred feet, but the front and the sides will go faster, since the wall can be shorter there. If you really can get a shopping cart from the Greek Market lady, we can get it done in four weeks."

"What about . . ." Jolene's hand drifted toward the community center.

"So . . ." Ware considered. He hadn't meant to quit

entirely, but he couldn't see himself going back, so there it was. "It's great there, of course. Lots of funnation. But I don't have to go."

Jolene puffed out her bangs and raised a pale eyebrow.

"My grandmother's in the hospital, and my parents don't want to have to worry about me, too. Being alone and having nothing to do. I'm not alone here, and there's plenty to do, so it's okay with them."

"What's she in the hospital for?"

"She fell. She broke her hips."

"Why'd she fall?"

"*Why?* No *why*. She just fell."

"People don't just *fall*." Jolene took off her hat and waved it around. "One minute you're standing, then boom, you're *down*, broken *bones*. Something happened. What happened?"

"Well . . . I don't know, I wasn't there." Ware turned his head. He felt a wave of revulsion sweep through him, as if he'd lifted a rock and found maggots. He'd been in a pool, floating around, waiting for some silly lights to come on. *Had* something happened to Big Deal? Something from her condition, being old? Something he should have protected her from?

He rolled away and tugged up some grass. "She broke both her hips and had to have them replaced. That's all."

Jolene propped herself up on her elbows and flung off her shades. Her eyes gleamed in a way that made Ware feel queasier. "What did they do with them?"

"With what?" he asked. Although he knew.

"Her old hips. The bones, right? I never thought about people parts."

"They got rid of them, I guess. It doesn't matter. We should get back to work."

"It doesn't matter?" Jolene's eyes bugged out at the depth of Ware's ignorance. "In lots of places, they just leave stuff out for buzzards or rats. How about that for your grandmother's old bones? Or how about landfills? People break in, looking for stuff they can sell. How about if someone found her hips, put them up for sale?"

"That couldn't happen. That would be terrible."

"Oh, right. I forgot, you live in Magic Fairness Land." She lay back and covered her face with her hat. "But here in the real world, bad things happen."

Ware jumped up. "Break's over. Back to work."

twenty-six

Ware gave Jolene the silent treatment, which she didn't seem to notice, for the rest of the morning. But when she pitched her tools into the hedge to leave, he found he didn't want to be alone. "So . . . you want to go home and make lunch? I'll wait."

"Not going home." She pulled out the garbage bag, then headed for the rear driveway. As she passed her compost piles, she waved toward them. "Need more stuff."

"Okay, wait. I'll go with you."

"Nope." And she was gone.

Ware retrieved his lunch, although he wasn't hungry, and climbed the tower. He forced down the peanut butter sandwiches, stiff and dry, and drank the juice, hot as soup.

In the heat, the banana had browned. He flung it hard

over the edge of the tower wall. As he watched it fall, he remembered: *People don't just* fall, Jolene said. Something had happened to Big Deal.

Ware had handwritten the Knights' Code in his report, on the last page, page eleven. It had taken so long to get it looking just right that he'd memorized all thirteen rules. Number three was: *Thou shalt respect all weaknesses and constitute thyself the defender of them.*

He hadn't constituted himself the defender of his own grandmother's weakness. "Big Deal, I notice you aren't feeling well today," he could have said. "Plus there's your condition of being pretty old. Let's call the doctor."

It would have been so easy.

Across the parking lot, the queen palms drooped as though they were ashamed for him.

Below, though, the growing wall gave him hope. The do-over moat would be full soon. He could be reborn. This time, besides being normal, he'd be the kind of kid who would notice when his grandmother wasn't feeling well. The kind of kid who would do something about it.

twenty-seven

One week later, the days had fallen into a routine.

In the mornings, when the three queen palms shaded Jolene's garden, Ware helped her. Jolene kept up a running lecture on the history of trash management, and Ware always cut her off when she suggested some horrific possibility for the disposal of Big Deal's old hip bones. Otherwise he liked being there.

The first papayas were studded with tiny fruits; the second crop was shooting leaves out left and right in their joy at escaping their cans and landing in the nice, rich compost. Another thirty ChipNutz cans had joined the forty-seven emptied ones, and Jolene had hammered nail holes into their bottoms and planted a seed in each. The seventy-seven brand-new papayas were already poking up little green nubs, as if they wanted to know what all the celebrating was about.

Once the shade left, it was wall time.

When Ware first offered Jolene his sunscreen, she looked at him as if it were a tube of warm spit, but after that she seemed to enjoy the wafting coconut scent as much as he did.

Together, they lassoed big hunks of masonry and dragged them over the edge. They kept the hose beside them and took long guzzles of the hot-rubber-tasting water when the heat blasting off the foundation parched their throats to sandpaper.

Jolene never gave up control of Mrs. Stavros's sledge-hammer, and Ware always pretended this was a painful injustice. In truth, he was relieved. What if he couldn't swing it?

Once Jolene had busted a hunk of wall into smaller blocks, his job was to wheel them away in the shopping cart, then stack them. He liked this best, fitting the blocks together, filling the gaps with plastic bags full of gravel and then sealing those in with the caulking he'd found in his shed.

Like Jolene's plants, the wall grew a little every day.

Quitting time was always around one o'clock, when Jolene headed off to the Greek Market with her garbage bag.

Ware always tried to go with her, and she always refused to allow it. The more she refused, the more he wanted to go.

"Why not?" he complained after a couple of days.

"Because I say."

"You can't make up the rules. It isn't fair."

Jolene rolled her eyes—"There you go again, Magic Fairness Land!"—and walked around him.

He gave up after that. For the rest of each afternoon, he felt alone, but it was the peaceful kind of alone, not the lonely kind. He ate his lunch in the tower, then overlapped the new stretch of wall with garbage bags filled with gravel. He worked on his stained-glass window, or cleared and mopped an area of floor. He finished the sundial and started building a throne.

Another week passed, same, same, same.

Then came Friday.

twenty-eight

Friday, Ware was in the tower when he heard a car pull up in front of the church.

The car was large and sleek, a serious-looking charcoal color. A man wearing a serious-looking charcoal-colored suit got out. Even from up in the tower, Ware could see that his shoes were extremely shiny.

This, he thought, was a good sign. Nobody with shoes that shiny would come into a lot this dirty.

The man didn't. He strode in a very purpose-driven way to the center of the construction fencing, set a briefcase on the sidewalk, and opened it.

He drew out a bright yellow sign and attached it to the chain-link fence. Then he snapped his briefcase shut, strode back to his car, and took off.

Ware ran down the stairs, over to Jolene. He pointed out to the street and she seemed to understand.

The bright yellow notice was attached to the fence top and bottom, as if it wasn't going anywhere.

PUBLIC AUCTION

Parcel #788
Zoned Commercial .75 Acre

COMING THIS FALL

Ware glanced at Jolene beside him. Her face wore a look of terror. He clutched his chest at the full hundred-arrow volley. "It's okay, Jolene. It's going to be okay."

Jolene shook her head at the empty words, kept on shaking it. After a moment, she turned and ran down the street to the backyard of the Greek Market. He watched her shove through the bushes and disappear.

Standing alone on the wrong side of the fence, Ware felt exposed. He climbed back over and headed up the front walkway in shock.

Everything looked different now. The wrecked church, the growing garden, the whole lot, all looked fragile. They looked as if they were begging for help.

His eye caught a flash of metal from under a holly bush near the drawbridge.

Ware crouched and found a surprise: an A-frame sandwich board. He dragged it free.

Spelled out in black plastic letters, on both sides of the sign, was a message: **BE NOT AFRAID**.

And it was back in his head: the fear on Jolene's face when she'd read the auction notice, complete with another *thunk* to his heart.

Ware carried the sign around to her garden and planted it beside her papayas.

BE NOT AFRAID, Jolene.

twenty-nine

"What's this supposed to mean?" Jolene's hands were balled on her hips.

Ware took a step back. "What it says. Don't be afraid."

Jolene's knuckles whitened. "Who says I'm afraid?"

"Come on. I saw your face when you read that sign."

She looked over to where the notice gleamed. Her whole skeleton seemed to collapse. "They'll never get ripe. I'll never sell them and get the money I need. I was so stupid." She kicked over a papaya seedling.

Ware hurried to tip up the can. He patted the soil around the little plant as best he could. "It isn't right. We made this such a good place."

Jolene shook her head in disgust. "Maybe in Magic Fairness Land the right thing happens. But not here."

She kicked over another can. "I'm not going to leave them here to get killed by a bulldozer. I'll do it myself."

"Stop it."

Jolene didn't. She kicked another one, and another. "And then I'll have to get some jobs."

"No, Jolene. We won't let it happen. You won't lose this garden."

"What are you talking about?"

What *was* he talking about?

Ware suddenly saw page eleven in his report. Number twelve seemed to be lit up. *Thou shalt be always the champion of the Right and the Good, against Injustice.*

That's what he was talking about.

This was Injustice, all right. He needed to be a champion of the Right and the Good.

This was, in fact, the purpose that would drive his life, he was suddenly certain.

He pulled himself up tall. "*I* won't let it happen, Jolene. *I* will save your garden."

Jolene snorted. "How are you going to do that?"

"I don't know yet. But I will. You won't lose your garden. I pledge."

"You *pledge*?"

"Promise. I promise."

"For real?"

"For real."

Jolene eyed him hard for a long time. Then she carefully righted the cans. Her hands, as she patted the plants back into place, looked like she was praying.

When she walked out of the lot, Ware was left alone with his vow.

It was an insane, impossible-to-keep promise, of course.

But he didn't care. Because when he'd made it, his heart—which, he suddenly understood, had been useless up until now, just killing time pumping his blood around—his heart had lifted right out of his chest, as if it had been reborn as a bird, and was now soaring somewhere near the top of the watchtower.

And the view from there was terrific.

thirty

Friday was different at home, too.

"You moved her into the rehab place?" Ware asked his mother when he found her in the kitchen. "Is she okay?"

"More than okay," she answered. "The doctors say she's healing well. And she's like her old self already. We hadn't been in the room an hour before she was telling the staff how to schedule her roommate's kidney dialysis. Who else but Big Deal, huh?"

The knot of worry Ware had been carrying loosened a little. "Actually, I can think of one other person. . . ."

"Fair enough, I guess I did inherit that gene," she admitted with a laugh. "Now, let me make you something to eat. I've missed you." She opened the fridge and frowned. "Not a fruit or vegetable in sight."

And with those words, Ware saw a complete side-flank strategy open up in the Greek Market battle, simple and Jolene-proof. "I'll get some," he offered casually. "There's a place near the Rec."

His mother dug a couple of twenties from her wallet. "No junk."

Ware scrubbed his hands, then sat and watched as she shook some crackers onto a plate and sliced some cheddar. "Where is this rehab place?" he asked when she joined him at the table. "Can I go see her?"

"'May,' not 'can.' It's downtown. You could take the bus after Rec, I suppose. I can't take you. I have zero free time. I'll stop in on my way home from work sometimes, but . . ." She dropped her head to her hands. "There's so much to figure out. Insurance. What to do about her furniture if she needs to move. The whole mess."

Ware put down his cracker. If something had happened to Big Deal, something about her condition, something he hadn't defended her from, that caused her to fall, then *the whole mess* was his fault.

"Well, it's nothing for you to worry about. Your uncle Cy and I will figure it out."

He swallowed hard. "No, Mom. You have to tell me about stuff like that."

They both startled at a soft thud of distant thunder. Ware glanced out the window. The sky looked bumpy and yellow, like the cantaloupes Jolene had tossed on her compost pile yesterday. Thunderstorm coming, right on schedule.

"I'm not kidding, Mom. You and Dad have to tell me things. I'm not some little kid anymore."

"Hey, watch it. You're not *some* little kid. You're *my* little kid. The only one I've got."

Ware didn't answer. His mother said that a lot. Always before, it made him feel treasured. But today it felt as if she'd wrapped a blanket over his face.

She reached over and ran a thumb around his forehead at the hairline. "You're filthy. What have you been doing?"

"So . . . we're gardening."

"We? Who's we?" she asked, brightening in such a hopeful way that Ware's heart fell.

"Mom, don't worry about me."

"Well, I do. Because . . ." She picked her napkin from her lap and folded it into a neat triangle. "When I was young, I was—"

"I know. Class president, a million friends. And Dad played three sports. I know."

"I just want you to be happy."

He thought about telling her that sometimes he was happy spending time alone. But no matter how many times he tried, she would never understand. He'd learned this the evening before his eighth birthday, when she had come barging into his room.

"Didn't you hear me calling you?" she'd asked, eyes panicked.

Ware scrambled to his feet, confused. He'd done something wrong, but what? "Sorry, I was . . ."

His mother charged around the room, snapping on his two lamps, the overhead light. Erasing the dramatic shadows that the low winter rays were casting on his ceiling. "Lying on the floor all alone in the dark? Why didn't you hear me? Do you know how worried I was? What were you doing?"

Her questions were coming too fast, or maybe his brain had slowed. "I was . . . thinking about eights."

"What?"

"Looking," he'd corrected himself. "Looking at how eights are really circles on circles." He hoped he'd gotten the right answer, the one that would ease the anxiety on his mother's face.

He hadn't.

"Looking isn't doing, Ware. What were you *doing*?"

"I was doing *in my mind*." He pointed to the ceiling, tried to show her how the swirls of plaster made an infinity of vertical infinity signs. "See?"

"Oh, Ware," she said, sinking onto the bed with her head in her hands. "I just want you to be happy."

Which had only confused him more. Lying on the floor, he'd actually been aware of the physical presence of happiness. It felt as if he'd swallowed a glowing seed. But his mother's face was so very sad.

"I'll try, Mom," he'd promised, meaning it. "I'll try more."

Three and a half years later, apparently he still hadn't tried enough.

"Do you think people can ever get a redo?" he asked. "If something's wrong with them, can they start over, like brand-new?"

"Oh. No, I'm afraid not. Your grandmother's prognosis is very good, but she won't be like new."

Ware suddenly felt alone. Not the peaceful kind of

alone, the lonely kind. He got up and brought his plate to the sink.

His mother rose, too. She went to the calendar. "Six more weeks until we own this house," she said.

They both jumped at a crack of thunder, close by. Ware went to the window. Black clouds were tumbling in.

His mother joined him. "It's going to be fine," she said, head pressed to the glass spattered with sudden rain.

Ware couldn't tell if she was talking to herself or to him. "It's going to be fine," she said again, as if whoever it was needed extra reassurance.

Ware thought about the new notice, his impossible vow, his grandmother falling on his watch.

"It's going to be okay."

He wasn't so sure.

thirty-one

The next day, Ware lay on his side watching Jolene swing the sledgehammer in a storm of concrete dust. He had stuck close to her all morning, afraid she was going to abandon the lot again. But she had worked hard hoeing a new trench, and Ware understood that the hoeing was a message: she'd decided to trust him. This felt like a miracle, and the miracle made him feel both relieved and anxious at the same time.

"Don't you think this lot should feel different?" he asked. He'd been wondering again about what made water holy, which was a thing he kept secret from Jolene, of course—they might not be enemies, but his plan to get reborn still felt too feathery and brave to risk sharing—when the question had expanded. "I mean, it was a church. Don't you think it should still feel different here?"

"I told you." Jolene slammed the hammer down. "They took all the holy with them."

"But what does holy even feel like? Do you think we'd notice if it came back?"

Above, the queen palms rustled a warning. Ware sat up. He heard the tight hiss of a bike braking and the clang of it tossed against the construction fencing.

He and Jolene watched Ashley drop down over the fencing and shake herself into composure. Her cool evaporated when she saw the operation in the parking lot. She hurried over.

"You can leave," Jolene said, leaning in threateningly. Her safety glasses made her look like a giant bug surveying a meal. "We're covering the pavement. With water. No more danger for those birds. So, bye."

Ashley looked skeptical.

Jolene dropped the hammer and yanked off the goggles.

Ware stepped between them. "It's true. We're building a wall around the foundation. We're making a moat."

"A *moat*? Like around a castle? That's, um, ridiculous?"

Ware turned away, face burning. Moats weren't ridiculous. Most people thought they only protected castles from ground-level approaches, but tunneling ambushes were much more dangerous, and a moat made those impossible.

"You want to be a knight in shining armor, big hero, chivalry and all that stuff?" Ashley went on.

Ware had to step away at that. *Knights were brave, they were loyal, they administered justice,* he recited to himself, stomping up the back steps. On top of that, they practically invented leading purpose-driven lives. From age seven their purpose was to train for knighthood. After they were knighted, it was to serve their liege lords.

The problem, he had to admit when he had climbed to the top of the tower, was the chivalry part.

Ware remembered the evening he'd handed his mother his report. "What a crock!" she'd sputtered.

Ware, sitting on the floor beside her chair as she read, had been crestfallen. "Mrs. Sprague didn't think it was a crock. I got an A."

"Oh, not your report. Your report is very good. But here?" She pointed to page eleven. "This business of protecting fair damsels? If the men hadn't deprived the

126

women of their rights in the first place, they wouldn't need to go showing off about how chivalrous they were! What a crock."

Her words had left him dismayed for days. If the Knights' Code no longer applied in today's world, that meant that he himself would never have a chance to exemplify its standards. To live a life of honor, of service to a liege lord. Most importantly, to come to the rescue of those in need.

Ware had stockpiled numerous imaginary scenarios for coming to the rescue of those in need. Due to his temporary lack of muscles, he populated them with people from the extreme ends of the age range: babies crawling into oncoming tidal waves; old people too weak to finish crossing the street. In each, he'd swoop in—chin up, chest out, advancing boldly—to pluck them from disaster's brink.

When he'd thought about it more rationally, he'd realized that it was only that one part about damsels that didn't apply. Nowadays, girls didn't need special treatment as if they were weaker—in fact, nowadays they'd be knights, too. All the rest of the code was still okay.

No, the real disappointment was that *he* never would

be a knight. He hadn't even protected his own grand-mother when she'd needed it. He'd promised to save a papaya garden from a bank but didn't have a clue how.

Now, everywhere he looked he saw the ridiculous-ness of his dreams reflected back at him. Even the queen palms seemed to be working hard to hold down a laugh.

Him, hero material?

What a crock.

Jolene's voice floated up. "You don't tell one single person about this place. Not one single word."

And then it struck him. He flew down the stairs, ran back to the girls.

"That's the whole deal?" Ashley was asking. "All I have to do is not tell anyone, and you'll actually cover all this pavement with water?"

"Yep," said Jolene.

"Nope," said Ware.

Both girls spun to him.

"You're going to do one more thing."

"Oh? What's that?" Ashley said.

"Get your father to order the bank not to auction this place."

"Please. I don't think so."

Ware grabbed his thigh and grimaced. "All those broken crane legs . . ."

Ashley crossed her arms. "Fine. You actually make a moat here and I'll talk to my father." She walked off, ponytail swinging.

Jolene's eyebrows took a hike up above her sunglasses.

And in their mirrors, Ware saw himself again. A kid who was not quite so pathetic after all.

thirty-two

Ware had never seen the Greek Market before, because it faced Second Street and his mother had determined that First Street was the most efficient route downtown, and once she'd determined the most efficient route anywhere, she never wavered.

When Ware grew up, he'd take a different route every time he went somewhere.

Anyway, there it was right next door behind the east wooden fence. A sign over the awning announced *Greek Market* in gold letters, in case he'd missed it, but he wouldn't have. For a moment, he could only stand outside on the sidewalk and stare.

As Ware headed into kindergarten, his parents had staggered him with a superdeluxe box of 128 crayons.

All those colors displaying themselves in a rainbow of promise, all for him.

He felt the same joy of abundance now. Fruits and vegetables burst out of their bins, so bright they seemed to be lit from within. *You see that? Wow!* he would have said. Except as always, who could he show?

Ware had left only ten minutes after Jolene, but she was nowhere in sight. Probably she was grabbing stuff from the dumpster. The question was, what did she do after that? She was never back by the time Ware left, so where did she spend the afternoons, dragging a bag of garbage?

Ware shook his head—he had an actual job to do here in the forbidden Greek Market—and stepped inside.

He picked up a basket and tossed in a package of blueberries and a head of lettuce, then carrots, tomatoes, bananas, and plums, then headed for the register.

"Hot one out there," he said to the checkout lady. Ware appreciated that for six months of the year, that was the greeting everyone gave whenever they went anywhere in Florida. It made things easier not to have to come up with an original opening line.

"Hot one out there, yes indeed," the lady agreed.

Ware placed his basket on the counter. Beside him, a crate of what looked like lumpy footballs, mottled green and orange, caught his attention.

He reached out to touch one, felt the leathery skin.

The sign on the bin had fallen over. Curious, he flipped it up: PAPAYAS, $1.99 a pound.

Papayas. Ware lifted one, felt its surprising weight.

"I know some papaya plants," he told the checkout lady, although he hadn't planned to add anything after the "hot one out there" opening. "They're pretty spindly."

"That so?" the checkout lady said.

Ware looked down doubtfully at the heavy fruit in his hand. "I don't know how they'll hold fifty of these."

"Things generally grow into what's needed of them," she said. "That is what they do."

"Do you really think so?"

"That has been my experience, yes, indeed." She took the papaya from him. As she leaned to the scale to weigh it, Ware glimpsed an open door behind her.

Outside was a garden. A woman with white-streaked hair piled on her head stood beside a table under an arbor of vines. She wore a flowered blouse and baggy trousers belted with twine. A girl with stringy yellow hair falling over faded overalls perched at the table.

Ware watched Jolene drink from a glass of purple juice and dig into a plate heaped with food.

The checkout lady straightened, blocking his view. Ware leaned to see around her.

"That'll be twenty-three twenty," the checkout lady said, thumping his purchases into a paper bag.

Ware craned his neck. The woman in the garden—Mrs. Stavros, it had to be—was pointing to the grapes above her head, and Jolene was nodding.

"Twenty-three twenty," the cashier repeated, one hand out, the other on her hip, teapot-style.

Ware rose on his toes, the closest he had to a watchtower. Mrs. Stavros dished more food onto Jolene's plate with a hand on her shoulder, and Jolene threw her head back and out came a sound Ware had never heard before.

It was a nice sound—gurgly and soft, like water bubbling out of a fountain. A real surprise coming from someone with such sharp elbows and knees. Someone with arrow-slit eyes.

If he'd been in an actual watchtower he might have toppled out. He hadn't known Jolene could laugh.

thirty-three

When Ware lowered himself from the oak limb that afternoon and saw the man at the bus stop, he nearly dropped the groceries.

It was the man's hair. Dark brown like his mother's, rippled and close-cut like his own.

He took a quick step behind the tree, but the man turned.

"Ware," he called, lifting his hand. "There you are."

Ware walked over on legs that suddenly didn't feel quite solid. "Uncle Cy. What are you doing here?"

Uncle Cy wagged a finger. "Wrong question, little man," he said with the kind of laugh that meant things weren't funny. At all. "The right question is, what are you doing *not* in there?" He nodded to the community center.

Ware opened his mouth, but nothing came out.

"I'll start." Uncle Cy patted the bench and Ware sank down. "Your mom asked me to pick you up. Imagine my surprise when I went inside and couldn't find my nephew."

Ware could imagine, all right. He dropped his head to his hands. "Did you ask?"

"I did. Some teenager. He pointed me to the sign-in sheet. No nephew today. No nephew all week."

Ware groaned. He peeked between his fingers. "You reported me? Missing, or something?"

"No. I almost called your mother, but then I remembered she said you took the three forty-five bus home each day. I thought: Hmm. She drops you off, you don't go in but you take the bus home. So I decided to wait here."

Ware raised his head. "I can't stand it, Uncle Cy. It's awful."

"Well, I saw that. When I was your age, I would have ditched that place, too. But hiding behind a tree all day long? That's not good, little man."

"I don't do that."

"I saw you, Ware. You came out from behind that big oak." Uncle Cy's voice was gentle but sad.

Ware stood up, hoisted the bag. "Come with me," he said. "I'll show you where I go."

thirty-four

U ncle Cy pulled a beer from the fridge and hopped onto the counter. He moved like a cat, lanky and cool.

Ware put the groceries away and poured himself some orange juice. "Are you going to tell them?" He stole a sideways glance at his uncle.

Uncle Cy rested his head on the cupboard. "What do you think?"

"No. Maybe. But please don't." Ware lifted himself onto the counter beside his uncle. He cupped his glass with both hands, hiding the silly seahorses that pranced around the rim. "My mom thinks I need more"—he lifted air-quote fingers from the cup—"Meaningful Social Interaction."

Uncle Cy sighed. "It's what she does, my little sister. Fixes things. Even things that don't need fixing. You don't seem like you need fixing to me."

The unexpected kindness of the words undid Ware. *He didn't seem like he needed fixing.* He felt himself on the verge of tears. "Unless she's right. Maybe there's something wrong with me."

Uncle Cy put down his beer. He took off his glasses and polished them on the belly of his shirt, then put them back on and looked at Ware expectantly.

And Ware surprised himself. He told his uncle all of it. How he felt different from other kids, kids who tumbled through life in packs, who jumped into the middle of whatever was going on. How he liked to watch from the edges for a while, do reconnaissance from the watchtower. And how he could spend hours by himself, making things or just thinking, and not be bored.

And then he told his uncle the worst. "She wishes she had a normal kid."

Uncle Cy frowned a tiny frown. "That's hard to believe. She talks about you all the time."

"It's true. She called me antisocial. Like I have a disease." He held his breath.

Uncle Cy steepled his long fingers to his lips. "Well, if that's a disease, I've had it all my life."

Ware swelled with so much hope he couldn't reply.

"Yeah." Uncle Cy nodded. "Just then, it sounded like you were describing me. Actually, it sounded like you were describing everyone I work with—the musicians, cinematographers, the writers. The whole tribe. Sounded like you were describing an artist."

And just as abruptly, Ware's hope was dashed. He looked at the floor. "I can't draw."

Uncle Cy shrugged. "Lots of kinds of artists, you know." He crossed his arms behind his head. "When you were just a rug rat, I came to see Big Deal. Your family was there, too. We were moving her into that Sunset Palms place. I took you out one day, get you out of your parents' hair, took you to the ocean. First time you'd seen it. You went rigid, as if you'd been electrified. Eyes like *this*. And you kept reaching for the water, wanting to drink it."

Ware felt a shock of recognition at the story, the way he felt whenever he passed a mirror unexpectedly.

But of course wanting to drink the ocean would sound crazy. Especially to people like Uncle Cy, who went to film festivals with celebrities, who was practically a celebrity himself, and who sent postcards from places like Morocco and Hong Kong and Calcutta, places you had to look up on a map. "I was a weird little kid, huh?"

"Weird? No. That's when I thought maybe you'd be an artist."

Ware gripped the counter. "What do you mean?"

"First time I knew it about myself, I was a kid, too. Maybe eight or nine. Friend of mine had a new kitten. Its paw pads were so perfect, like shiny little coffee beans. I had the urge to swallow them. That's when I knew. Not that I was an artist—I hadn't figured that out yet. Just that I was different, and this difference would be important my whole life."

"I don't understand."

"It's like this: artists see something that moves us, we need to take it in, make it part of ourselves. And then give it back to the world, translated, in a way the world can see it, too. That make sense?"

You see that? Wow. "Yes."

"Artists need solitude to do that. And quiet. By the way, you'll have to fight for that—the world loves noise."

Ware fell back against the cupboard. He hadn't realized how tightly he'd been holding himself since he'd uttered the word "antisocial" out loud. "I get it."

"I know you do. You showed me today."

"I did?"

"Your lot. The moat, the sundial, that stained-glass window. You're transforming it. That's what artists do."

Ware remembered his drawing of the escaping tiger. *Not everyone can be an artist.* "But that's not me. I told you—I can't draw. Or write or make music, or anything."

"The lot *is* your art right now. You're *creating* it." A slow smile spread over his face. "I have a hunch. Tell you what. I'm going to give you a movie camera. Nothing fancy, just the one I travel with. I'll show you how to use it, teach you how to do some easy editing. You bring that camera with you to the lot and film what you're doing there. I'll be back in a month—you show me."

"So . . . you won't tell my parents?"

"Sorry, little man. I think I have to. Or you do."

"No. If they knew, my dad would worry. My job this summer is to not worry them. And besides, Mom would send me back to Rec, and then Jolene would be alone with everything. I've made a promise to her. Please."

Uncle Cy rubbed his forehead, eyes squeezed shut. Then he slid off the counter. "All right. The community center is next door. Go there if anything happens, or if you even think something's not right. You stay safe."

Just then, the door opened and Ware's mother walked in. "Evening, you two. Having a nice chat?"

"Evening, Little Deal." Uncle Cy hugged his sister. "We are, in fact."

Ware's mom poured some iced tea and sat at the table.

Uncle Cy raised his beer like a toast. "Got some good news for you tonight, Little Deal." He winked at Ware.

"Oh? What's that?"

"Turns out you're raising an artist."

She lifted her eyebrows toward Ware. "That so?"

"That's so. Know what that makes you?"

She shook her head, sipped some tea. "What's that make me, Cyrus?"

Uncle Cy beamed. "Lucky."

That night, Ware cut up the papaya and passed it around for dessert.

"It's good, right?" he asked after everyone had had some. "Really sweet."

"It is," his uncle agreed. "Extremely sweet."

"Plus smooth. It's a very smooth fruit, don't you think?"

"Yes, Ware. It's remarkably smooth," his mother said, giving him a funny look.

"It tastes kind of like a cantaloupe, but more cantaloupey, right?"

His father cocked his head. "Did you grow this yourself? Are you a papaya farmer now or something?"

Ware dipped his face, but he smiled to himself. He was a papaya farmer now. Or something.

thirty-five

A camera lens reveals how special things are, even things that appear ordinary. The way you could walk all day on a beach full of gray stones, but it's only when you pick one up and study it on your palm that you notice how there isn't another one like it.

Everything begged to be filmed, to get that attention. "Don't worry, you'll cut out anything extra once you know your story," Uncle Cy had advised. "First, film whatever you want."

"What are you going to put in your movie?" Jolene asked, the first day.

Ware stopped to think before he answered. "Whatever moves me."

"Moves you?"

"Whatever makes me feel something. That's what I'll film."

And that was what he did.

He filmed Jolene easing a cylinder of soil from a ChipNutz can, so carefully the sprout in the middle never wobbled, and patting it into place in the trench. He filmed her hoisting Mrs. Stavros's hammer over her head, smashing it down true. He filmed her fist-pumping at the crack, every time.

He filmed a line of ants carrying tiny bits of watermelon away from the compost pile; a frayed green ribbon fluttering from the flattened slide. He sorted through the boxes of photographs and took out the scenes that castle ladies would have chosen for their tapestries. He lined them up and zoomed in on each. He chose a single papaya and shot a close-up of it every day. "You're going to be a star," he'd promised the lucky plant. "Going to grow up right on camera."

Before long, the camera felt like part of Ware's body. Each day, he would have kept on filming right past the bus if his alarm hadn't gone off. And when he got home, he went straight to the computer to see what he'd caught.

Lighting was an issue: some things looked washed out

under the glaring sun; things in the shade weren't bright enough. A piece of poster board solved both problems: used to block the sun like a visor, or covered in tinfoil as a reflector. The poster board also made a great backdrop for subjects that had seemed lost. He wrapped his T-shirt over the camera's microphone when street noise interfered and began to experiment with the buttons—focus, frame rate, white balance.

By the end of the week, the film was matching what his mind imagined. *You see that? Wow,* every frame seemed to say.

Uncle Cy had said the hardest part would be editing. "You have to leave a lot of great stuff on the cutting-room floor."

Ware wasn't ready to edit yet, because he didn't know his story. But Uncle Cy had talked a lot about *dramatic turning points*, and he hoped he was getting some of those.

"I wish I'd seen the wrecking ball," he said to Jolene one day.

"Nuh-uh, you don't. It was awful."

"Okay, maybe I don't. But I wish I had that film."

Jolene shrugged. "It was on the news. You could probably look it up."

That afternoon, Ware did. Not only was there news footage, but people in the crowd had posted clips, too.

Jolene was right. It was awful. Swing, crash, BOOM. A cannon to the heart every time.

But it moved him.

He put the camera up to the computer screen, and he filmed.

thirty-six

Ware sat on a cinder block, chin on his palms. Uncle Cy had said he was transforming the lot, but was he?

The old playground was a thriving garden now. He'd raked the overgrown grass of the front lawn into medieval designs. He'd finished the stained-glass window and was making a suit of armor out of some beat-up cookware and a roll of tinfoil. The moat wall was rising and would soon be full of water. But right in the middle, the wrecked building was wrong.

The shape was fine, castle-like already with its tower and chunky walls. It was the color. Pink was all wrong for a castle. Castles rose from the surrounding land, made from its native materials. Clay, stone. Castles were the color of rocks.

Rocks.

Ware got up and walked over to Jolene's garden. He kicked at the mountain of lousy dirt Jolene had dug out of her trenches. "What did you call this stuff?"

"Rock dust. It's useless."

"Maybe not."

He went up into the church and gathered a dented spaghetti pot, a mixing spoon, and a mop. He filled the pot with rock dust, hosed in some water, and stirred.

He lugged the pot down to the west wall of the church, still in the shade, and began smearing the slurry onto a patch of wall. As soon as it was pasted on, it slid down, leaving a sick pink track.

If the mud slid off in the dry air, how would it ever hold up through a summer of evening rains?

Ware remembered a sand sculpture exhibition he'd gone to the year before. "Elmer's glue," the winner had whispered behind her hand, when he'd asked how it held together. "Mix it in with the water."

He went back up into the church and retrieved a whole case of glue. The labels read *Shure-Stuck*, not *Elmer's*, but glue was glue.

He mixed it in and started over, painting the sticky

mud on with the mop. Every once in a while, he noticed that Jolene got up and made a show of stretching, but he knew she was spying on him.

It kept him going.

Two hours later, stopping only to film his progress, he'd covered the entire wall up to where he could reach.

He solved the problem of the high parts in medieval style. He had just finished setting up the Y-shaped branch, the bungee cords, and the colander when Jolene gave up spying and came over.

She studied the mudded church wall. "You're insane," she said matter-of-factly, as if reporting that the sky was blue.

Ware stepped back and saw what she saw. "I guess so," he had to agree.

"I mean, really. This is exactly what's wrong with you."

"You're probably right."

She pointed at the catapult.

"Basically, a giant slingshot," he mumbled, head down.

"Show me."

Ware filled a couple of sandwich bags with the mud,

placed them in the colander, pulled back, and let them fly. The baggies burst against the church wall with a satisfying *splat*.

"*Literally* insane."

"I know."

Jolene shook her head with a tragic eye roll. Then she pushed him aside. "I'd better help."

Jolene, it turned out, was a catapult natural. But even with two of them hurling stucco bombs, it took a while. The noon sun was just peeking over the ramparts when the final brown splat covered the final pink spot.

They walked back to his block and sat on it together.

Instead of smooth and pink, the west face of the church was rough and stone-colored, convincingly medieval. A few of the baggies had stuck, resulting in random glossy patches that reflected the sunlight in a jaunty way.

"Wow," Jolene said.

"Wow," Ware agreed.

"Don't castles have flags?" Jolene asked after another minute of reverent admiration.

"They do." Cut into triangles, run through with sticks, the red-checkered tablecloths would be perfect. As Ware imagined them snapping from the castle parapets, he suddenly saw knights dashing below them on armored steeds, heard the clash of broadswords, and smelled pigs roasting over smoky fires.

Jolene poked him. "I said, people would see them from the street."

"Oh, I was drifting off. Sorry."

Ware caught himself. It wasn't true. He wasn't sorry. "I was drifting off," he repeated, "and it was great. But you're right, no flags."

"And you can't mud up the front of the church."

That one was harder. "No," he promised at last. "Not yet."

thirty-seven

The next morning, Ware hung out on the oak branch for an extra moment, admiring the mudded wall. The church now looked strong and defiant, like the best castles, like a fist of rock bursting up through the ground.

As he was about to drop into the lot, he heard the squeal of car brakes. The squeal sounded urgent. Also familiar.

He glanced back. He stifled a panicked gasp.

His mother.

Ware ducked deeper into the leaves and watched. She shut off the engine, and when she turned to open the car door, he dropped from the branch and darted behind the bus kiosk.

His mother slung her bag over her shoulder and

started up the walkway to the community center door at an extremely purpose-driven pace. It looked like the purpose was to find out if her son was where he was supposed to be.

"Mom," he yelled. "Over here!"

She turned, a hand shielding her eyes. "Ware!"

Ware hurried to intercept her on the walkway. This would be a lot worse inside with all the Rec kids watching.

"Ware, I got to the end of the street and I realized—"

"I know, I know," he began, hands raised.

"—that I didn't give you an August bus pass. I was worried you'd . . ." She pulled a new pass from her bag. "Wait. What do mean, you know?"

"So . . ." He looked back at the oak. How could he even begin?

A clanging at the bike rack bought him some time. A girl locked her bike and then skipped up the walk. Ware raised a hand. The girl looked at him strangely, but she waved back and Ware breathed.

"Oh, my goodness," his mother said. "You realized it too! You thought, 'It's August first, how will I get home today?' so you went over to the bus stop to figure it out!"

"Actually . . ." Ware searched his mother's face. The little lines that had creased her forehead all summer had relaxed. "Right," he said. "I thought, 'Hey, maybe there's a sign in there or something.'"

She reached out as if to stroke his face, then pulled back as if she remembered how old he was.

Just then, a car pulled up to the curb. The tall-necked boy, Ben, got out. He leaned down and smiled into the car at the driver.

And once more, Ware recognized himself in Ben and winced. Because the smile Ben wore was the same one he used to flash every day he'd been dropped off here, at least the days he'd actually gone inside. *Don't worry, I'm fine,* the smile said. *Super popular, just like all the other kids.* Why didn't anyone else see how fake it was?

The tall-necked boy's smile, when he turned and saw Ware, was real.

"Hey, Ben," Ware said, smiling back.

"Hey," Ben said. "See you inside."

Ware turned back to his mother and took the bus pass. "I should go."

His mother took a step and then stopped. "You've changed so much this summer. You're like a new person."

Ware was caught off guard. "I'm really trying to do that, Mom. Be a new person. I know you want me to change."

"I see that. You're happy every morning when I drop you off here. You haven't complained about Rec once. You're making friends here. And it's as if you've changed inside, too."

"You think so?"

"Well, thinking ahead about the bus pass? It's as if you're more *here*."

"What do you mean, *here*?"

"You know. You were always . . . kind of off in your own world."

Off in your own world. His mother had never said that before, at least not in that blaming way, as if it was something he should be ashamed of. Someone else had said it that way recently—he didn't remember who, but he hadn't liked it then, either.

He *had* changed this summer. He was spending more time off in his own world. And it turned out, he didn't feel ashamed about it. Turned out, he really liked it there.

thirty-eight

Back in the Middle Ages, moats were disgusting, Ware knew. A moat was basically the castle's sewer. But this was no ordinary moat they were making. This was an enormous, circular get-yourself-reborn tub. And whatever holy water was, the one thing it wasn't was dirty.

"It's almost time to fill the moat," he broached the subject with Jolene. "We need to put in some filter plants now, to keep it clean."

Jolene shrugged. "We promised to cover the pavement with water. Nobody said anything about it being clean." She drove another nail hole into the ChipNutz can on her lap.

"But you don't want dirty water near your papayas, do you? We need those filter plants."

"The garden is uphill. Don't care."

"Dirty water might attract rats."

Jolene raised her hammer and bared her teeth. She looked like something rats should be afraid of.

Ware wasn't giving up, but he was temporarily out of arguments. He picked up a can. Another pile of them had appeared overnight. "Where do you get these?"

Jolene hitched a shoulder to the Grotto Bar. "Walter."

"What are they, anyway? The picture on the cans looks like bark. What do they taste like?"

Jolene wobbled the hammer in the air, as if asking the universe for help. "They taste, they taste . . . like bacon and peanuts and french fries, all at the same time."

That sounded too good to be true. He put the can down and picked up his cause again.

"Polluted water will smell awful. And if it smells, someone will complain. And if someone complains . . ."

"Oh, all right!" Jolene got to her feet. She slapped on her hat and holstered her trowel. "What kind of plants?"

Ware began to list the ones he'd found in his research. But when Jolene blew out her bangs with an impatient puff after just a few examples, he quit. "Basically, we need the kind that grows where there's water sometimes, but sometimes not."

"Well, I know a place like that," Jolene grumbled, as if she were admitting it at gunpoint. "Behind the school. It's got water after it rains, but then it goes dry."

"Sounds like a detention pond. Let's go see it."

Jolene said okay, but then she ducked into the hedge.

"I meant today," Ware called.

Jolene reappeared, patted the bib of her overalls, then trotted down to the front of the lot.

Ware followed and they climbed over the fence.

Jolene stopped at the notice. She shuddered.

"It's going to be okay," Ware said. "We'll make the moat, and then Ashley will get her father to stop the auction." He nodded as if it were a great plan.

But inside he wondered.

thirty-nine

Jolene stuck her pointer finger through the chain-link fence.

Ware peered down the slope. An oval pond nestled alongside a road. "That's a detention pond, all right. I can see the overflow grate from here. That plant down there, whatever it is, that's what we need." He worked a sneaker toe into the wire and scaled the fence.

At the marshy edge of the water, he crouched and splayed a little plant across his fingers. "Waterweed," he announced.

"Looks like the stuff in aquariums," Jolene said, coming up behind him.

Ware nodded gloomily. "That's probably where we'd have to get it—a pet supply place. I hope we can buy enough. I only have forty-seven dollars."

"*Buy* enough?" Jolene sputtered. She slid her black garbage bag out of her bib pocket and produced her trowel.

Ware batted them away. "That's stealing!" he hissed.

Jolene snorted. She fell to her knees and troweled out a ragged circle of turf, then dropped the clump, ripe with the scent of mud, into the bag.

Ware jumped into guard position between Jolene and the road. "Okay, but if anyone stops us, we'll put it all back."

"No one will stop us."

And Jolene was right—no one did. Not that trip, and not on the other three trips they made, although Ware's heart pounded every step. "You know what this bag looks like it's full of? A human body, that's what," he warned each time. "You'd better hope we don't get stopped by the police."

"You spend a lot of time imagining things that aren't going to happen," Jolene said.

Ware thought he heard a hint of admiration in the complaint. Of course, maybe he imagined it.

They tucked the tufts around the edges of the

foundation. Jolene donated a shovelful of compost to feed each clump, but you could see how it cost her.

"We have to water them now," she said.

"Maybe not." Ware pointed to the sky. Piles of black clouds were rolling in from the west. Evening thunderstorm, coming early.

He glanced over at the community center. It was dry inside, but . . .

He saw Jolene look up at the door at the top of the stairs beside the Grotto Bar's sign. He knew she was weighing the same trade-off about her apartment.

"Nope," he said. "Follow me."

Jolene shot him a skeptical look, but she followed him onto the foundation and over to the big kitchen table. A crack of lightning split the dark sky, and she scrambled under.

Ware hurried over to the wall of closets. He grabbed a couple of tablecloths and the box with the candle stubs and lighter, and ran back.

He draped the cloths over the table, weighted them with bricks, and ducked in as the first drops hit his shoulders.

Jolene sat with her knees drawn up to her chin.

"*Under the Table,*" she said in a voice that clearly implied both capitalization and italics, as if she were christening the spot. She watched as one by one he melted the candles' bases and stuck them to the floor in an arc on his left side, an arc on Jolene's right, and then lit them all.

Rain drummed on the tabletop. Wind gusted shingles around the deck and flickered the candles. A curl of air blew a fresh earth smell from Jolene's garden into the wax-scented cave. Ware pulled the tablecloth snug. "Think your papayas will be okay? They're kind of . . . floppy."

"Sometimes it's good to be floppy. The wind can't snap you."

A lightning bolt struck so close that the air under the table flared silver. The smell changed to something blue and electric. Thunder cracked, a deep thud Ware felt in his chest. He edged the slightest bit closer to Jolene.

The arcs of candles surrounded them like parentheses. As if he and Jolene were extra information.

"Extra information," he risked, eyes on his knees. "My parents wish they had a different kid."

"Extra information," Jolene replied, as if she understood parentheses, too. "My aunt wishes she didn't have a kid at all."

forty

"Cutworms." Jolene glowered down at the papayas she'd planted a few days before. Half of them were crumpled to the ground. She let out a string of swears.

"I don't think you should say those things here," Ware muttered.

"I told you, the holy's gone." She swore again. "They're chewing through the stems. Mrs. Stavros says I need collars around them. She says make the collars out of paper cups. Do you have any?"

"Maybe." Ware climbed onto the foundation and rummaged through the kitchen junk. He trotted back with a box labeled *Communion Cups*. "Are they too small?"

"Nuh-uh. Cutworms are caterpillars. Caterpillars

have pretty short legs." She handed Ware a rusty knife. "Cut off the bottoms, slit the sides."

Ware placed one of the miniature plastic cups on a cinder block and started sawing.

Jolene knelt and troweled out a dandelion, then carried it over to the front walkway to transplant. "They're nice flowers. Not their fault they got born in the wrong place," she'd answered when he first asked her about it. "They shouldn't get killed for it."

Ware thought the dandelion saving was ridiculous, but he did like how it dressed up the front of his castle.

A minute later, she came back. "Know how they got rid of trash in New York City, back in the day?"

Ware wasn't in the mood. He bent over his knife. Dripping sweat stung his eyes, the blade was dull, and the cups too slippery. He was wrecking about half the ones he attempted.

"Pigs, that's how," Jolene said, as if he'd begged her to go on. "Like, on Mondays, the people in one neighborhood threw their garbage into the street and the city sent a herd of pigs through. On Tuesdays, another neighborhood. Like that."

"Well, great," Ware said, not looking up. "How

many of these do you need? I'm getting a blister."

"Great? *Great?* No, not so great *for the pigs.* Can you imagine the kind of stuff people threw away back then?"

Ware shrugged and kept on butchering cups. Communion cups were supposed to hold the blood of Jesus—he knew that much. He dropped the knife and looked up at the queen palms. They seemed to shake their fronds in disapproval.

"Jolene, do you ever think the holiness is still here, but it's hiding? And we're supposed to find it?"

Jolene smacked his sneaker with her trowel. "How would a pig know if someone threw out something poisonous?"

Ware went back to his sawing.

"Or gross. Like . . ."

Ware realized too late where she was heading.

"Like a *human hip*?"

He finally looked at her. "You're obsessed."

"Yes!" She was beaming in smug victory. "So give up. Call her and ask her where they are."

"I can't. She's at some rehab place near here, but she doesn't have a phone." Ware poked at the new blister, raw on the ball of his thumb.

Jolene sat back on her heels. "Is that where they took them out?"

Surrounded by mutilated communion cups, Ware felt uneasy at the question. "No. That was somewhere else. She's just there now."

"Well, what about other people there? Do they have stuff gone?"

Ware squirmed. "Her roommate only has one kidney. But maybe she was born without the other one."

Jolene's eyes lit up. "A kidney," she mused. "Anyone else?"

Nothing good would come from answering Jolene's question. Ware knew this. But he'd overheard his mother tell his father something last night, and out it came. "An old guy there is missing a leg. He rolls his wheelchair over to my grandmother at lunch and invites her to go horizontal dancing. She throws her Jell-O at him."

Jolene dropped the cup she was holding. "A hip, a kidney, *and* a leg?" she demanded. "All in one place?"

Ware nodded again. He squeezed his eyes shut and waited.

"Get the address," Jolene said. "We go there tomorrow."

forty-one

"What? What's so interesting about a candy bar wrapper?"

Jolene flattened the wrapper on the bench as carefully as if it were a treasure map.

Ware pulled his cap down. He'd been nervous every minute since Jolene's decision, worrying about everything that could go wrong. As long as Jolene and Big Deal never met, he reassured himself for the hundredth time, things would probably be fine.

He risked a glance back at the community center. At noontime Ms. Sanchez should be busy trying to keep milk carton missiles from launching, but you never knew.

Beside him, Jolene bent over the wrapper.

"There was a cat that lived next door once," he said.

"He used to stare at the wall. For hours. We think he must have been hit on the head when he was a kitten." Number five in the Knights' Code was: *Thou shalt never give wanton offense.* Ware knew he was giving wanton offense right now, but he couldn't help it.

Jolene placed a finger on the wrapper. She raised her head. Her sunglasses looked like discs of ice. "Or maybe he was a genius cat. Maybe he figured out that if he stared at the wall long enough, you'd quit bothering him, let him be a cat, instead of wanting him to be something else."

Ware checked his watch. Still two minutes before the bus. "I wouldn't do that. I don't do that."

"Yes, you do. You want a wrecked church to be a castle. You want a bunch of busted cookie sheets to be a suit of armor. I saw that screen—you want some broken glass to be a jewel-y window. You want the world to be fair, when it's not."

Ware couldn't argue the last point. He did want the world to be fair. It wasn't fair that more people didn't want the world to be fair. "You think my window looks jewel-y?"

Jolene smoothed the wrapper, bent even closer.

"Seriously. What are you doing?"

She sputtered up her bangs. "I'm trying to know where this has been. Before. Like, did the paper come from an apple tree way up north? This blue color, did it come from turquoise out west? Everything was something else before. Sometimes, if you look hard enough, you can see it. The whole story of a thing."

The bus fumed up then. Jolene dropped the wrapper in the trash. Ware followed her onto the bus, thinking. He watched the buildings roll by, each built of things that used to be something else.

"Jolene, if everything was something else before, then everything will be something else afterward."

"Of course. Recycling."

"Even people."

"Especially people."

forty-two

Everything was something else before and will be something else after. The concept had expanded so explosively in his brain on the bus ride that Ware forgot to worry about bringing Jolene to the rehab place.

As soon as he walked into the bright lobby of the New Horizons Rehabilitation Center, though, he remembered. He aimed a warning look over his shoulder.

Jolene raised clasped hands to her chin and fluttered her lids innocently. Which was the opposite of reassuring.

"We're here to visit my grandmother," he told the woman behind the registration desk, who was eating an egg salad sandwich.

The woman paused with her sandwich in midair. She wore a pale blue scarf splotched with yellow stains, as if she ate egg salad sandwiches a lot. Her eyes were squinty chips behind crinkly black lashes. It looked as if she was peering at him through a nest of spiders.

"My grandmother. We're here to visit her," Ware repeated. Then he gave her Big Deal's name. Spiders made him nervous.

The woman put down her sandwich. "Isn't that the nicest thing." Somehow, she made it sound as if what she really meant was *Now, here's a big pain in the neck, just when I'm trying to have my lunch.* She pushed a clipboard across the desk. "Sign in here."

Ware filled in their names, then turned.

Jolene was halfway through the lobby. Ware dropped the pen and caught up with her.

"No fooling around. You're just here to get that . . . *information* you want. Now, we should meet back in the lobby by—"

"Trash can!" Jolene pointed down a side hall.

And she was off.

forty-three

Ware stood in the doorway, overwhelmed by how much he'd missed his grandmother.

The beds in the room had metal rails, like giant cribs. Lying in hers, Big Deal looked too small, like a wrinkled baby. Her hair, which until this moment he had not suspected was a wig, hung off a lamp on the bedside table. Her scalp was covered with soft gray fuzz, as if the wrinkled baby were dusty.

As she whuffled a small snore, the skin on her neck trembled. The tremble hurt something in his chest. He hadn't constituted himself the defender of his grandmother's weakness when it counted, but he could do it now. He tiptoed in and eased the sheet up to her chin.

Big Deal startled awake. "Oh, Ware! What a nice surprise." She looked toward the door.

"I came by myself. Mom's working a million hours."

"She is. They both are. Poor them." Big Deal plucked her wig off the lamp and tugged it on. She looked like herself instantly. The magic of hair.

"I'm sorry I left you alone that night, Big Deal," he plunged in. "I should have known you might fall. I should have—"

Big Deal waved it off. "That's ridiculous. How could you have known?"

How could he have known? That was the question, all right. "I wish I had, though. Maybe you wouldn't be here now. Is it terrible here, Big Deal?"

"Oh, no, it's all right here." Big Deal craned her head toward the door. "Although a person would think she could get a little bacon now and then," she added, loud enough that a passing orderly chuckled.

Ware dropped into the red plastic chair beside the bed. He tipped his head to the other crib. "Where's your roommate?"

"Dialysis."

He pointed to what looked like a television screen

behind his grandmother, glowing with squiggly lines. "What's that?"

"That? Oh, that's proof."

"Proof?"

"That I'm alive. I got a little dizzy this morning, so they hooked me up. This is the kind of place"—she leaned to the door again and cupped a hand around her mouth—"*the kind of place where you can't get any bacon*, where you need to prove you're alive. Hand me my bag, would you, Ware?"

Ware passed her the purse, and she dug around until she found a lipstick. While she was applying it, he thought about the kind of place that would require a person to prove she was alive. Not a good one. "Were you scared?"

"You mean about this?" She patted her sides.

Ware nodded.

"I suppose a bit. But then your mother came. It helps a lot not to be alone. Also Mrs. Sauer—she barely left my side. She visits me twice a week, too. That's something—a two-hour drive, each way."

Ware scowled, then quickly rearranged his face.

"I saw that look. What do you have against Rita?"

Ware twitched. "*She* has something against *me*."

Big Deal waved a hand. "Oh, she's a little vinegary is all."

Ware knew he should drop it. He was here to make his grandmother feel better, not get her stirred up. But number eight in the Knights' Code was *Thou shalt do battle against unfairness whenever faced with it*, and he was faced with it now. "What about those twin girls visiting next door? Mrs. Sauer made them a cake. I saw her bring it over. So she's nice to girls."

Big Deal patted the sheet until she found the bed remote. She pressed a button and rose majestically until she was looking right in Ware's face. "Those girls were quiet. Barely came outside, except to make a puzzle on the patio the one time. Who knows, maybe Rita likes quiet and out of sight is all."

Ware tapped his fingers on the chair arm. He really should let it go, but he couldn't. "No. I think she doesn't like *me*." Suddenly, he remembered who it was who'd said *Off in his own world* about him in that blaming way. Mrs. Sauer, when he'd climbed out of the pool. "She acted as if I'd done something wrong, Big Deal."

"If you think that, you should ask her next time you

see her. Now, speaking of girls who are quiet and out of sight, who's your friend?"

Ware felt himself redden. "My friend?"

"The one who's been skulking around the hall the whole time you've been here, peeking in. Overalls, blond, could use a meal."

Ware got up and leaned into the hall. There was no sign of Jolene. "You saw her?"

"See those mirrors up high?"

He looked up. He nodded.

"They're so the orderlies can see the gurneys coming around the corner, avoid crack-ups. I may have accidentally adjusted a couple with my cane. I see everything that happens on this floor."

"Oh. Well, she did come with me, but she's not my friend. And she's sure not quiet."

"No?" Big Deal seemed to grow larger, as if she weren't going to fit in that crib much longer. "Well, go call her in, the little skulker. Let's hear what she has to say for herself."

Ware sighed, but he got up. There was no talking Big Deal out of something once she'd decided.

He found Jolene hanging out of a dumpster in back

of the building. He tugged her overalls and she slid to the ground.

She held her arm up to display a sling as if it were a diamond bracelet. "Just thrown away. People."

"My grandmother sent me to get you. I can say you left."

"She wants to see me?" Jolene pulled off the sling and stuffed it into her pocket.

"She's kind of *direct*," Ware warned. "She wants to know everything."

"Me too," Jolene said. "Maybe I'll finally get some answers."

forty-four

Jolene was a whole lot more polite than Ware had guessed she could be. "Pleased to meet you, hot one out there today, what did they do with your old hip? Ma'am. Er . . . please," she said after the introductions.

Big Deal tugged her wig around, as if it was suddenly too tight. "Well, hmm. I had those hips for seventy-one years. I don't know why I didn't think to ask where they were taking them."

"That's all right, ma'am," Jolene said, all soothing comfort. "But can you ask now? Thank you, please."

Big Deal shook her head with what looked like genuine regret. "The surgery was in a hospital back home. I'm only recuperating here. Now, tell me why you want to know." She raised her eyebrows at Jolene.

"Uh-oh," Ware muttered.

Big Deal shot him a look that reminded him he used to be afraid of her. She smiled encouragingly at Jolene.

Unbelievable. His own grandmother, taking the side of a stranger she'd known for a single minute.

Jolene sat up primly. "Things get used up or broken. Or they're too hard to take care of. But that doesn't mean they're trash. I like to know if something gets thrown away it's done right. Respectful-like. Ma'am."

Big Deal nodded. "Very admirable."

Jolene raised her chin toward the empty bed. "How about, excuse me, your roommate? Do you know where her kidney went?"

"Sorry. The subject hasn't arisen. But I'll tell you what. There's a fellow here knows things. Name of Franklin, goes around delivering meals and rustling up blankets. He used to work in a big hospital over in Tampa. Go find Franklin—you'll get some answers."

Jolene mumbled a string of thank-you-ma'ams and bolted.

"She's obsessed with how stuff gets thrown away," Ware said apologetically when she was gone. "It's like she thinks trash has feelings."

Big Deal perked up. "Why is that?"

Ware shrugged.

"You haven't asked?"

"Ha!" was all he could manage at that terrible idea.

Big Deal cocked her head. "Girlfriend trouble?"

"No, she's not my . . . she lives behind the community center. I only help her with her gardening. That's all." He got up and looked out the window. This line of questioning could bring him dangerously close to the subject of where he spent his days. "That's a nice tree down there. Have you seen that tree?"

"What's her family like?"

"She lives with her aunt. I'll bet a lot of birds land in that tree. Did you know that a sandhill crane weighs ten pounds and it lands feet-first?"

"An aunt? What about her parents?"

"I don't know. All I know about it is that her aunt doesn't want her there."

Big Deal sat up. "That is terrible. That is a crime. Why doesn't she?"

Ware spread his hands.

"Ware, there is a considerable lot you don't know about a person who came all the way here with you."

"It's just . . . Jolene. If she wanted to tell me something, she'd tell me."

"That sounds like an assumption, Ware. Don't make assumptions about people. Maybe she can't guess that you're interested. It's never wrong to ask."

Ware pondered the idea. Maybe he'd try. Probably not.

He pulled the chair out, but Big Deal waved him away.

"You go catch up with her. I'm tired. But come visit again. And bring her with you." Big Deal lowered the bed and nestled her head into the pillow. The proof machine beeped in a reassuring manner. She closed her eyes and smiled. "Little skulker."

Ware could still hear her chuckling as the elevator door closed.

forty-five

Ware checked the waterweeds every morning for a week. The new plants didn't seem upset they'd been kidnapped, but they didn't seem thrilled about it either. He filmed them each day, and each day they looked the same: wet and green.

The new wall grew taller around them, like an anxious crowd rising on their toes to see better. When it was finished, Ware stalled. "Three feet is a lot of water. A lot of pressure," he said. "We need a back-up wall around this deep part, just in case."

They built the second wall inside the first, leaving a gap that they filled with garbage-bagged gravel. And each day that week, too, Ware checked the waterweeds.

Still wet and green.

Ware thought about the proof machine in his grandmother's room. He would like to have one above those waterweeds.

And then finally, finally, he noticed something different. He scrolled back to the first day he'd filmed them to be sure, then ran to get Jolene. "See here on the fringes?" he asked. "How the green is lighter?"

Jolene dropped to her knees and raised her sunglasses to inspect them closer. "Yep. They're growing again."

"They're growing again!" he crowed, two fists in the air. "We did it. Life!"

Jolene blew her bangs out and rolled her eyes. "It's not like you invented growing," she scoffed. But she was fighting a smile.

He gave a sprig of waterweed a gentle tug, and the little plant held firm. *I'm not going anywhere*, it seemed to say. *I like it right here.*

"It's time," he declared. "Let's fill the moat."

forty-six

"You never asked? All this time, you never *asked*?"

"It's water. Water's free."

Ware folded his arms and narrowed his eyes.

"Okay, fine," Jolene said. "We'll go ask Walter."

Ware looked up at the *Grotto Bar* sign. The flamingo's beak suddenly looked extremely sharp. "We?"

Now Jolene folded *her* arms and narrowed *her* eyes.

"Okay. We." Ware followed Jolene over the fence and across the parking lot. Jolene pulled open the back door and marched in, but Ware stopped to prepare himself. He was walking into a bar. An actual bar. He wanted to etch every detail into his memory.

The bar was cool and dark. While his eyes adjusted, he drew in the smells—beer and something that smelled like it used to be beer. And then the sounds—whirring fans, clacking billiard balls, a song that seemed to consist entirely of the words "Without youuuuuu . . ."

The bar itself was an L-shaped island of wood. A mirror behind it reflected hundreds of bottles.

And two kids. Jolene looked like herself, but Ware was embarrassed to see that he could have been auditioning for a roller-coaster commercial. He closed his mouth and blinked his eyeballs back into their sockets.

A bear-sized man behind the bar was filling a mug from a tap built into the mirror. His head was shaved and a rainbow tattoo encircled his neck like a halo that had slipped. He glanced up in the mirror and winked at Jolene. "Hey, Sprout," he said over his shoulder. "You and your friend pull up a stool. I'll be right there."

Just in time, Ware saw that this was a joke, since the stools were bolted to the floor. He chuckled in what he hoped was a manly way.

Jolene shot him a puzzled look. She climbed onto a stool and he took the one beside her.

The bartender came up and leaned in. His hands, splayed on the bar, were the size of baseball mitts. "The usual?" he asked.

When Jolene nodded, he grabbed two mugs and shot something pale and sparkling into them from a spigot. He arranged a couple of orange slices on the rims and set the mugs down on coasters that said, hilariously, *Bottoms Up!*

"Walter, can we have some water?" Jolene asked.

Walter tipped his head to Ware. "Who's we?"

"This is Ware. I told you about him."

"Good to meet you, Ware," Walter said. He picked up two more mugs and made for the sink.

"No, I mean outside," Jolene stopped him. "Can we have some water from your hose?"

"Of course, Sprout. It's hot out there. Take as much as you want—you don't have to ask."

Jolene shot Ware a look of triumph, and Ware picked up his mug. His first drink in a bar. Ginger ale. It tasted completely different, way better than any ginger ale he'd ever had. Possibly it was champagne.

When Jolene bent to her drink, Walter stretched and peered at the booths along the far wall. Ware thought he looked a little worried, but then Walter leaned in toward Jolene with a smile. "Got some more cans for you out in the stockroom. While you're out there, flatten the boxes for me, take them out to recycling, okay?"

Jolene grabbed her mug and pushed through a set of swinging doors.

A bald man at the far end of the bar raised a hand. "Hey, Walter. Fill 'er up," he called.

While Walter was gone, Ware swiveled to check out the customers. Four men playing pool, two guys in green uniforms hunkered over beer mugs a few stools away, two older women perched at a high-top table playing cards.

Counting the bald man, nine people.

Just then, another woman's head rose over the back of a booth. Her hair sprang out in a crown—the yellowest Ware had ever seen, but black at the center. She took a sip from a green bottle, swept a slow gaze around the place, and then plopped back down as if what she'd seen had exhausted her.

So there were ten of them—a dozen counting himself and Jolene. It had looked like more, because of all the mirrors. People in bars must really like to look at themselves, Ware concluded, because besides the giant mirror behind the bar, the walls were covered with them, all advertising beers in ornate golden letters. Some of the mirrors were also clocks. Ware was surprised that people would want to look at themselves with time sweeping over their faces, but there were many mysteries about bars he had yet to unravel.

He twirled his stool back to the bar and noticed what he'd missed before: blue plastic bowls were spaced every couple of feet.

ChipNutz. At last. He reached for the closest bowl, but just then Walter came back.

"Sorry. My client had a sensitive issue that needed my ears." Walter tugged his ear. "Professional listener. Mostly, that's my job. And, of course, every so often to offer a refreshing beverage."

Ware pointed to the bowl down the line. "And ChipNutz." He secretly pinched the side of his thigh. He was in an actual bar, having a conversation with an actual bartender.

Walter snapped his fingers. "Yes! Never underestimate the value of having something to crunch when you're trying to clarify a problem."

Walter picked up a white towel and began to polish the wood in slow, perfect circles. "Say you come in. I get you something to drink, then I ask, 'How you doin', pal?' You take a sip, then you say, 'Doin' okay, Walter, thanks. But I got this problem.' Now, do you have a problem, Ware?"

Ware nodded vigorously. He had several, in fact. His mother, Jolene, Mrs. Sauer.

"Okay, so here's where the ChipNutz come in." He slid a blue bowl over to Ware. "Take a handful and shake them into your mouth. Crunch for a while, and think about the problem."

Ware shook a handful into his mouth. And just as Jolene had claimed, they did taste like bacon and french fries and peanuts all at the same time. They were the most delicious thing he had ever eaten. He crunched them thoughtfully.

And Walter was right, it did help him clarify his problem.

"People have a lot of expectations about me. My mother expects me to be like her. She hates spending time alone, so she thinks it's bad for me, too," he began. "But I'm not her."

"Hoo, boy. Tell me about it." Walter nodded in a manner that somehow expressed sympathy over all the injustices of the world.

Ware munched another handful of ChipNutz and

was just about to venture into the subject of the vow he'd made to Jolene when she pushed through the swinging doors.

She peered around an armload of cans and nodded toward the exit.

Ware drained his soda, then drew out his wallet.

Walter waved it away. "On the house, pal."

"Thanks, Walter," Ware said in a new, deeper voice, and slipped off the stool.

Ware unscrewed the hose nozzle. For a moment, he and Jolene stared down at the water running into the vast, empty moat.

"Maybe it's not turned all the way on?" he asked hopefully.

Jolene shook her head. "Full force."

He followed Jolene's gaze as she lifted it from the hose to her papayas, and then to the front fencing where the auction notice was. He could read her feelings as if they were printed on his own heart.

"Everything takes too long," she said. "Except the things that don't take long enough."

"Hoo, boy," Ware said. "Tell me about it."

forty-seven

Jolene drew out a knife and sliced a papaya plant off at its base.

Sitting beside the plants, Ware dropped his movie camera and grabbed his ankles.

"Only the females make fruit," Jolene explained. "You can't tell which they are until they make flowers. See here? The male flowers spray out, kind of stringy. The females have fatter flowers, close to the base."

Ware looked over at the rest of the plants, happily growing with no idea that half of them were wasting their time. "So . . . what? The ones that turn out to be boys—I mean males—you kill them all?"

"Almost all. I keep a few around for pollination." She hacked down another plant. The plant fell over with a cry of betrayal only Ware seemed to hear.

"It's not their fault they can't make fruit," he tried. "They shouldn't have to die for it. Maybe you could plant them somewhere else."

Jolene shook her head. "You can't transplant a papaya. Their roots don't like to be disturbed. That's why I start them in cans. When I know which ones to keep, I can slide them out—that doesn't cut any roots." She glanced up at her apartment. "Once some people start growing in a place, they don't want to get kicked out."

Ware knew she'd meant to say plants, not people, but right now, he didn't care. "Well, it's not fair."

Jolene put down her knife. She smiled with goofy wonderment and smacked her forehead. "I keep forgetting! We're in Magic Fairness Land!" Then she frowned a clowny sad face and smacked her forehead again. "Oh, no, darn. Still here in the real world."

Ware felt a growl—an actual growl—rumble in his chest. "Why do you even care? So what if I live in Magic Fairness Land?"

Jolene cut off another stalk with a savage slice. "You're not a realist—you want things to be magically what they're not. You have to be a realist to survive in this world."

Ware shifted uncomfortably. "What do you mean, survive?"

"Make it through. Life. Life's going to crush you if you don't see it coming."

Ware looked around. It didn't help that he was surrounded by flattened playground equipment. This lot hadn't seen it coming.

"What should I do?"

"Open your eyes. Look out for life, coming to crush you."

Ware got up and walked down to the moat.

Jolene was probably right. She usually was. She'd been right about the baptistery—he'd looked it up that first night. He'd checked about those rakers and the Black Plague—she'd been right about that, too. And about people breaking into landfills, and about nobody caring if you stole waterweed, and about bar water being free to take.

Jolene was right about everything. So he needed to get reborn, not just as someone whose report cards said, *Ware is outgoing and normal!* and who lived a purpose-driven life and watched over his grandmother, but also as someone who could open his eyes, see life coming to crush him. A realist.

He lifted the hose that was filling the enormous do-over tub. The water, as far as he could tell, was just plain water. According to Jolene, the preacher had said some important words over it to make it holy.

He and Jolene were the closest the lot had to a preacher now. The water actually came from the Grotto, so Walter should have a say, too.

He gave Jolene's words first. "Everything was something else before."

"Hoo, boy," he added for Walter. "Tell me about it."

He thought for a minute about what would be his own contribution. "The outside is part of the inside when it's people," he said at last. Maybe the words weren't important, but they were the truth.

forty-eight

For three days and three nights, the water ran.

When Ware arrived at the lot on the fourth morning, he nearly fell off the oak branch, the way he had on the very first day.

Ware turned on the camera. He dropped to the ground and flew across the yard. He turned off the hose, then ran up the drawbridge.

They'd done it. Instead of crane-killing pavement, the church was actually encircled with harmless water. It gleamed like liquid sapphires in the camera lens.

Ware wished there were a seat behind him, because suddenly he really needed to sit down. Then he realized something pretty great: there *was* a seat behind him.

There were rows of seats behind him, in fact. Great

long rows of seats, long enough for a whole flock of people to sit on, ready-made for admiring the wonder of things.

He located the end of a pew and began plowing off shingles and boards and screens and insulation and chunks of concrete. When he'd cleared off a couple of feet, he kept going, because number five in the Knights' Code was: *Thou shalt persevere to the end in any enterprise begun.*

He cleared off the whole thing, and then he went to the janitor's closet and got some rags and cleaner. He polished the wood until it shone.

And then he sat down dead center. On the back of the pew in front of him was a brass plaque, carved with the word *BEHOLD!* It seemed to be an order.

Ware folded his hands together on his lap. He lifted his gaze to where the moat sparkled through the gaps in the wall. And he beheld.

forty-nine

"**B**ehold!" Ware ordered Jolene when she got there. But Jolene had been beholding since she'd run into the lot.

"Wow," she breathed as she settled herself on the pew beside him. "And it's not leaking?"

"A few places. I'll patch it. We'll keep the hose trickling. Plus it rains every day."

As if to prove him right, a bank of dark clouds drifted toward them, trailing veils of rain.

This was lucky, because Ware had something to ask, and *Under the Table* Jolene would answer. *Under the Table* she took off her sunglasses and he could see right into her soul.

He got up and led the way. "You said the people went

198

back to their old ways after they got dunked. Like going to the bar. How did you know that?" he asked when the candles were lit.

Jolene shifted. "I only said one did."

"But how did you know?"

"My window is over the bar's parking lot."

"Okay, but how did you know about the rest? Hitting their kids, you said. Drinking the rent?" Ware looked right into her eyes. He looked into her soul.

And he saw something terrible hiding there. He learned who the one person was. "Your aunt."

Jolene put up her dukes, cartoon fierce. "I'm almost bigger than she is."

Ware found his arms curling, too. As if they were a team. "And drinking the rent?"

"When my papayas are ripe, we'll always have the money."

Ware was struck silent for a moment. He hadn't known Jolene's home was at stake. "You won't lose your garden," he said, hoping he sounded more sure than he felt.

Jolene nodded. "I can't lose my garden." Then she leaned in and squinted right into *his* eyes. She looked as if she were trying to see into *his* soul. "How come you're so interested, anyway? Are you trying to get yourself *reborn*?"

Ware turned away. He could use some mirrored sunglasses right now. Or a pair of nictitating membranes.

He kept his gaze on the candles. "Of course not. It's all stupid anyway. A do-over tub, ha. Saints and angels and all of it."

"Right. Except for saints."

Ware laughed. "I thought you were a realist?"

Jolene shrugged. "Saints are real. I see one every day."

The instant Jolene left for the Greek Market, Ware marched down to the moat. He started to peel off his shirt, but he remembered in time. *The preacher dunks them, clothes and all.*

He waded to the deepest part of the moat. He took a moment and made himself perfectly still.

Make me a different person, he wished, as hard as he could. *Make me normal.*

He filled his lungs and fell back as hopefully, as start-overly, as possible. He kept his eyes closed, because it felt wrong to be looking around, enjoying the view, at a life-changing time like this. Then he got up.

Ware assessed himself. He felt cooler. Less dusty. His mosquito bites didn't itch. But did he feel different *inside*?

No, he did not. He felt exactly the same.

He heaved himself out of the water and climbed the back steps.

And there, dripping pools of water onto the church floor, he realized: He *did* feel different. For the first time ever in the lot, he felt sad.

fifty

"My father says he can't tell a bank what to do. He's only a city councilman."

Swing, crash, *BOOM*. Ware actually grunted at the blow as his ruined pledge crumbled to dust, and beside him Jolene staggered a step back.

He straightened up and mustered a protest. "But we covered the pavement with water. Look! Those cranes can't get hurt now. That was the deal."

"Um . . . a city councilman?" Ashley repeated. "That's a person that does *city* stuff, like programs and budgets?"

At that, Ware felt a very small click in his brain. Like a tiny key being inserted into a good idea.

Before he could pursue it, Jolene interrupted his thought. "It's *who*. Your father is a person *who* does city stuff. Unless your father is a thing, not a person? Is he a thing?"

Jolene's attack surprised Ware, but it shouldn't have. Sometimes when castle defenders threw down rocks on an attacking enemy, the enemy picked them up and threw them back. He just hadn't ever thought of grammar as a weapon.

"My father is a person," Ashley said, recovering. "But he's not the head of the bank."

Jolene shot her a look like a lance, steely and sharp. "Basically useless." She smashed a mosquito.

Just then a flock of white birds floated down. They began leading a purpose-driven march up the slope to the papayas on long pink legs, pecking the ground with long pink bills.

Jolene flung off her hat, revving up for a charge.

Ashley stepped in front of her. "Hold on. You want those ibises here. They eat bugs."

"Cutworms?" Jolene demanded. "Will they eat cutworms?"

"Are they worms? Then, sure. They eat worms."

"They're caterpillars."

"Um . . . caterpillars? Like popcorn."

Jolene settled back. But Ware could see she was going to keep a sharp eye on those ibises. Those ibises weren't going to get away with anything.

Ashley hurried after the flock. "You birds," Ware heard her comfort them. "This is your place. I'll keep guard."

Jolene turned to him. "Now what? 'I pledge,' you said. 'Ashley will get her father to stop the auction,' you said. Some plan."

Ware swallowed hard. "Well, that was plan A," he agreed. "Plan B might be a little different."

Luckily, Ashley came back down before Jolene could ask what plan B was. She swatted around her head. "Birds would help with these mosquitoes, too. A single purple martin will eat a thousand mosquitoes a day."

"Hope some show up, then." Ware scratched at a bite on his arm. "They've been terrible this week."

"Well, duh . . . standing water?" Ashley swept a hand toward the moat. "You made a mosquito factory here."

Standing water.

Of course. Each week Ware's father tore around the yard, upending every leaf and bottle cap that might hold a drop.

204

"So if the water moves, the eggs can't hatch, right?"

Number two on page eleven of his report: *Thou shalt always be prepared to help others in need.*

This was his moment. He was prepared.

He lifted his jaw and thrust out his chest. He stripped off his shirt and leaped boldly into the water.

Chivalry. Not such a crock, after all.

fifty-one

For the next few days, coming up with plan B occupied much of Ware's time.

It was extremely satisfying work. Most of the scenarios involved chaining himself to the ruined church or lying down in front of Jolene's papayas when the bulldozers came to scrape the lot. He'd face those machines down—ideally, surrounded by a crowd of breathless admirers, including a national television crew—unafraid in the face of the danger.

In all the scenarios, the machines backed off. Jolene's admiration would know no bounds. She'd laugh her soft gurgling laugh. Maybe she'd even hold his hand again.

But there was a problem, he knew. Even if he had the courage to follow through—which was not entirely certain—his parents surely held strict positions against a kid challenging a bulldozer, especially if that kid was the only one they had. Overprotection: one of the many disadvantages of being an only child.

Since forever, Ware had wished for a sibling.

Didn't matter which, brother or sister. His mother wouldn't have a spare minute to hang over him, she'd be so busy scheduling feedings and nap times and diaper changes, and then, later, playdates and ballet classes and ninja camps.

This brother or sister would be nuts about sports, too, so his father would finally have the kid he wanted sitting next to him on the couch instead of a boy who couldn't remember the difference between innings, sets, and quarters.

Or maybe it would go the other way. Maybe the new kid would be an even worse disappointment than he was. *We should have appreciated Ware more*, his parents would realize. *He's terrific just the way he is.*

The only problem with having a sibling would be his room. His room was the one place on the planet he had some privacy. When he closed the door, every cell in his body sighed in relief. He didn't think he'd survive if he couldn't have his own room. But still, he wished he had a sibling. Since forever.

Ware shook himself back. He had a plan B to come up with.

Sometimes he felt as if the answer was right there, in front of his eyes. Right at his fingertips. But the only thing in front of his eyes and at his fingertips was a secondhand, nothing-special movie camera.

fifty-two

Birds, with their height advantage, discovered the moat right away. Ware liked imagining the first one doing a cartoon double take in midair—feet braked out, wings wheeling backward—then spreading the word.

The word spread quickly. A giant heron floated in to stalk the wall, a pair of cormorants paddled the circuit, and a flock of what looked like black-and-white scissors skimmed the shallow end, all on the same day.

The next day, a chattering of wild parakeets settled in the three queen palms like bright little limes. After that, they came every morning and stayed for a few minutes, squawking a ruckus over every move he and Jolene made.

Soon after the birds came other animals: rabbits and

frogs, chipmunks and squirrels, dragonflies, beetles, and toads.

A full week after the moat was filled, a comically perfect latecomer crawled into the lot. Ware got down on his belly beside the turtle, his camera pressed to his face. "What took you so long?"

The turtle raised its head in a stately arc, looked straight into the lens, and blinked one eye.

Ware tapped the turtle's shell with a blade of grass. "I dub thee Sir Wink. You are welcome here."

Not all the visitors were. One morning Jolene discovered that the newest contributions to her compost had been swiped. What looked like tiny human handprints led to the moat.

"Raccoons," Ware identified the culprits. "They like to rinse their food."

He lashed together five window screens and settled the cage over the pile, then weighted it with a board. "You can lift it off, but the raccoons can't."

Jolene blew her bangs out and studied him. And for just a second he saw, reflected in those mirror glasses, a kid who was kind of okay.

fifty-three

Ashley started showing up most mornings. She said it was because she liked digging, and maybe that was true. Hand her a shovel and she always looked ready to burst into song.

But Ware noticed that what she was really doing was making the lot into a sanctuary for birds. She scattered the worms they turned up like little presents, and she piled bread crumbs and raisins and sunflower seeds on the moat wall. One day, he saw her sprinkling a trail of something red all around the lot. "Cayenne pepper," she explained. "Cats hate it? On their paws?"

Ware liked having her around. He liked how clean she always looked. How when a speck of dirt did get on her, it somehow looked intentional, like a piece of jewelry.

Most of all, he liked how she ended her sentences on an up note, making them sound like questions even when they weren't. It made you feel included, as if she wanted your opinion on things.

Jolene, however, picked fights with her whenever she could. It began to bother Ware more and more.

"My great-great-great-great-grandfathers tried to kill each other once," he told Jolene one day.

That got her attention. "Why'd they do that?"

"Well, because of the Civil War. They were on different sides. But they didn't know about me. That they were going to have something in common."

"You think Ashley and I are going to have a kid together someday?"

"Maybe. But no—I mean, maybe you have something in common with her that you don't know about yet."

Jolene sputtered out her bangs at that stupid idea.

"What do you have against her, anyway?"

Jolene peeled off her giant leather work gloves and tossed them to the ground. The move reminded Ware of knights throwing down their gauntlets to issue a challenge to battle.

"She lives in Magic Fairness Land, like you. Whenever she doesn't like something, her daddy fixes it. Except, unlike you, she actually gets to live there. Because she's rich."

Ware thought it over. He picked up the gloves, the sign that he accepted the challenge. "But her father didn't fix anything. She helps here at the lot herself, and she has other places she's working on, too. Getting them lit up, for those cranes."

"Oh, it's not for those cranes. Why would a rich girl care about birds?"

"Maybe because she cares about birds."

"Nuh-uh. It's probably for a school project. Or maybe she's going to write an essay about how great she is, saving them, so she can look good for college."

That sounds like an assumption. You shouldn't make assumptions about people. Ware heard Big Deal's advice in his head. But he gave Jolene her gloves back, the sign he wouldn't fight anymore. Jolene knew how the world worked. She was usually right. Still, he hoped she was wrong this time.

fifty-four

"Mm-hmm . . ." Uncle Cy leaned in closer to the screen. "Mm-hmm . . ."

When he'd arrived after visiting Big Deal, he'd only dumped his bag on the sofa before asking to see Ware's film. Since then, he'd been scrolling back and forth, reviewing.

While his uncle studied the screen, Ware studied his uncle. Silver-rimmed glasses, a silver stud in his left ear. Black jeans, a black T-shirt made of something silky, not rough like his own.

Ware's mother made him get new clothes for school every fall. He'd ask for black jeans and T-shirts. She'd never let him get his ear pierced, but he'd try.

Finally, Uncle Cy paused the film and leaned back.

He pointed to the screen. "You keep cutting to those three palm trees."

Ware didn't know if this was a compliment or a criticism. "Well, they're always there," he explained. "Everything else in the lot is always changing."

"But see? They change, too." He scrolled back. "Like here, they're sunny and languid. All's good. Then after we see the auction notice, you cut to them whipping around like they're distraught. How come?"

Ware made a mental note to use words like "languid" and "distraught" more often. "The bank's going to sell the lot. All our work gone."

Ware took a gulp of air. Saying it out loud made it real. Uncle Cy waited patiently while he got himself under control.

"I figure I could build something in the backyard once we own it, but Jolene really needs her garden. I've promised her I'll save it, but I don't know how yet."

"I'm sorry," Uncle Cy said. "But I meant the palms. Why are you doing that with them?"

"That's how I see them," Ware admitted. "It seems like they're reacting to what we do."

Uncle Cy nodded. "A Greek chorus. That's what I thought."

"I know it's dumb, just imagining . . ."

"No, not dumb. A Greek chorus is a device from ancient storytelling. In a play, it's a group of people in the wings who comment on what's going on. They let the audience know what emotion is expected. See? You're a storyteller."

"No, because I didn't mean to do it."

"Exactly. You did it intuitively. I called it. You're a filmmaker."

Ware had to laugh. "That's crazy. Filmmakers are people like you. Not kids like me."

"People like me were all kids like you, once."

Ware tried, but the closest he could get to an image of his uncle as a kid was a smaller version of his grown self. Cool, semifamous, black jeans and an ear stud. "What were you like at my age?"

Uncle rubbed his back against the chair. The move reminded Ware again of a cat, lanky and cool. He scratched his own back on his chair to test out the move.

"So . . . I remember I was always trying to explain myself," Uncle Cy said. "I used to drift off, and then I'd apologize, as if I'd done something I needed to apologize for. People thought I was lazy, or stupid or stuck-up. I had a really hard time in school."

"That's weird. You're a hero in school now. Last winter our grade watched the documentary you did in the refugee camp with all those little kids following you around. I got to tell everyone you were my uncle."

"Thanks."

"Half the kids were crying. They gave their allowances, they held a fund-raiser afterward. That must feel good."

"Well, it's great when that happens, sure. But it doesn't happen like that very often. You never know who will see your work, and you can't predict how they'll react. Plus that's not why you make it."

"Then why?"

"Because it needs to be made, and you're the one to do it."

Ware lay in his bed that night, staring at the ceiling. Tonight, the plaster swirls didn't look like infinity signs. They looked like question marks. Question marks inside question marks on top of question marks.

fifty-five

Two days later, Uncle Cy left and a tropical storm arrived. It planted itself a hundred miles west in the Gulf, like a toddler throwing a weather tantrum.

"It's supposed to be like this through Wednesday," Ware said at breakfast on Monday when it began. "They won't let us outside at Rec. You know how unhealthy the air is in there. I should stay home." He added a subtle cough.

It was a long-shot argument he hadn't expected to win, but his parents, weakened from two sleep-deprived months, didn't even put up a fight.

"Fine, whatever, could you run the vacuum?" his mother had said as she staggered off to work.

"And maybe a load of laundry," his father added,

scooping up his keys.

And so Ware had three whole days to work on his film. Which, if he had to title it the way it was, would definitely be called *Jolene's Hands*.

Jolene's Hands would have been a pretty good movie. But it wasn't the movie he was meant to make. That was what had come to him as he was drifting off under the question-mark ceiling plaster.

He was meant to make the story of the lot. Because it needed to be made, and he was the one to do it.

But for another reason too.

Uncle Cy had said that it didn't often happen that your film made people do what you wanted. That meant that sometimes it *did* happen. And this, he decided, was one of those times. People would see this film and cry and empty their wallets. He'd bring it to school in September. Other schools, too.

This film would save the lot.

Ware cut most of the footage of Jolene's hands. Most, but not all. Then he went to work.

At the end of those three days, his back ached, his fingers were cramped, and his eyes were red and dry, but he felt better than he had ever felt in his entire life.

And he had managed to trim nearly sixteen hours of footage to four minutes and forty-two seconds.

Those four minutes and forty-two seconds began with the photo of the church being built and ran all the way up to a family of ducks floating in the brimming moat. In between, a wrecking ball smashed down the roof, papayas grew in time-lapse frenzy, and castle walls were mudded. He patched in Jolene's dandelion bed and her compost pile, his sundial and the church floor emerging as he swept off the debris, and a new stained-glass window spilling its rainbow rays.

Even Wink got a close-up—winking, of course.

He stood and stretched wide. He cracked his knuckles and shook his neck loose. He poured a ginger ale, dropped in a slice of orange, and took a long drink. Then he popped an extra-strength honey-lemon cough drop into his mouth.

He was ready for the final layer.

"Everything was something else before," he began to voice-over his film. "And everything will be something else after. Sometimes, if you look hard enough, you can see it—the whole story of a thing."

fifty-six

"So? Plan B?"

Ware shifted away from Jolene on the bus seat. It was Thursday, and he hadn't seen her since Sunday, and he'd missed her—which had come as a very big surprise to him—so he'd been glad when she decided to come along to see Big Deal. But now he was reconsidering. "Uh-huh," he agreed. "Plan B."

"Well, what is it?" Jolene pressed.

"So . . ." Plan B was a little unformed. Plan B had some holes. But the fall was a long way off. "Just trust me. It's going to work. But I can't tell you."

"Why not?"

"Because I say."

Hearing her own words seemed to take Jolene aback

for a second. Ware changed the subject while he was ahead. "Why are you even coming? I thought that Franklin guy told you what you wanted to know."

"He did. The parts that don't get recycled into other people are 'disposed of in a most respectful manner.'"

"Well, don't you believe him?"

"I believe him." Jolene licked her thumb and rubbed at a scuff mark on the back of the bus seat in front of her. "This used to be a cow," she said, as if that explained anything.

She peered at the seat more closely. "Or maybe some detergent bottles. It's too dirty to tell."

"Jolene. Why are you coming?"

She looked up, wide-eyed. "You said your grandmother *asked* me to," she answered, as if catering to the whims of the elderly were a natural result of her thoughtful personality. "Also, you were gone this week. I got kind of bored."

Ware felt a little buzzy. As if he might be glowing. Jolene had missed him, too.

Just then the bus rocked a hard turn. A can of Chip-Nutz rolled out of the Winn-Dixie bag at Jolene's feet.

Ware caught it and held it up.

Jolene shrugged. "Your grandmother wants bacon. They taste like bacon."

Ware handed her the can. "I didn't tell you she wanted bacon. How did you know?"

"I heard last time."

"You heard her?"

"Oh, everybody heard her," Jolene assured him. "The whole place."

Ware cringed, his hand to his face.

"Let me tell you, if I had a grandmother," Jolene muttered, rubbing the scuff mark again, "I'd want someone with a voice that everyone could hear."

Ware sat back. He hadn't known Jolene didn't have a grandmother. It wasn't fair. He really hated unfairness.

Which reminded him. "That thing you say. About me living in Magic Fairness Land. You're wrong." The insight had come to him the night before. He had lain awake practicing the announcement. "I mean, you're right that I don't think you should just take it when bad things happen. But I don't want things to be magically what they're not. I want them to be what they *could be*. And somebody has to want that, or nothing bad will ever get better."

Jolene blew her bangs out with an unimpressed sputter. "Besides, you do it too."

Jolene lifted her shades and arrow-slitted her eyes. "I do not. I'm a realist."

"Nope. That papaya you got from the Greek Market. Everybody saw a rotten piece of fruit. You saw a plantation."

Jolene crossed her arms and turned to the window. The whole way to the Bright Horizons Rehabilitation Center, she didn't turn back once.

fifty-seven

Inside, the same woman sat at the desk eating an egg salad sandwich, wearing the same stained scarf. She squinted up at them from her spider-nest eyes and said the same words—"Isn't that the nicest thing"—when Ware told her why they were there. She didn't seem to mean it any more this time around.

Ware signed them in, wondering if he had somehow traveled backward in time.

But just then, something new and surprising happened. A woman in a yellow pantsuit marched out of the elevator and through the lobby. She moved as if she led an extremely purpose-driven life, and that purpose was to get the heck out of the New Horizons Rehabilitation Center.

"You go ahead," Ware told Jolene. "I'll see you up there."

He caught up with the woman at the doors. "Mrs. Sauer. Wait."

Mrs. Sauer turned. She frowned.

Ware drew a deep breath and plunged in. "Why don't you like me? My grandmother said I should ask."

"I don't *not* like you, young man." She crossed her arms over her chest. Because of her thinness, and the yellowness of her pantsuit, it made Ware think of two pencils crossed over a slightly thicker pencil. Somehow, the pencils felt sharpened.

"I think you're mad at me because I wasn't watching her. I should have been. But I didn't know. About her condition. If I'd known, I would have—"

Mrs. Sauer looked disbelieving. "How could you not know about her condition? She's your grandmother."

"Well, I knew. I just didn't know I was supposed to watch her because she's old."

"Because she's *old*?"

Ware nodded. "Her condition. Being old."

"Being *old*? Your grandmother has diabetes, young man."

226

"Diabetes? *My* grandmother?"

Mrs. Sauer drew herself up and pursed her already pursed lips. She seemed to be asking the question, *How could he not know?* and then answering it herself: *Off in his own world.*

But that wasn't it.

"What a bunch of nonsense! No one *told* you?" she asked with an indignant huff.

Ware shook his head.

"Well, that is just plain *wrong.* It's diabetes, for Pete's sake, not the Black Plague. I've had it for twenty years. Half the people I know have it. You should have been told."

She crossed her arms over her chest again. This time, though, her thinness and the yellowness of her pantsuit reminded Ware of sunbeams. Sunbeams of justice.

"That simply wasn't fair to you," she went on. "You are not a child, and you needed to know. I just hate unfairness, don't you?"

And Big Deal was right: it helped a lot not to be alone.

fifty-eight

W are stood at the door and looked in through its window.

Unbelievable. Jolene was perched on the bed beside Big Deal, directly below a sign on the wall that read, "Visitors: Please Do Not Sit on the Bed." Both of them were digging into the ChipNutz can between them as if they hadn't eaten in weeks.

He opened the door.

"Tastes like bacon!" Big Deal crowed, holding up a nugget between freshly fuchsia'd nails. She winked and patted the bed.

Ware came in and sat, as pointedly as he could, on the chair.

"You just missed Rita, Ware." Big Deal licked a

crumb off her lips. "You could have cleared things up with her."

Ware looked down at his lap. "I talked to her," he said carefully.

"Oh, good. And?"

Ware pressed his lips together. He glanced at Jolene and then at the door.

Big Deal patted Jolene's hand. "Do me a favor, would you, dear? Go find Franklin, tell him I could use another blanket."

Jolene hurried off on her mission.

Big Deal turned to Ware. "And?"

He gripped the chair arms so hard his fingers whitened. "And she *was* mad at me. And I don't blame her. You didn't feel great, and I left you alone and went out to the pool. I'm really sorry about that. But why didn't you tell me you had diabetes?"

Big Deal looked down at her nails.

"She's not mad at *me* anymore. She's mad at *you*."

"I expect she would be."

"It's just diabetes, for Pete's sake. It's not the Black Plague."

Big Deal nodded her agreement.

And then he understood. "My mother didn't let you tell me, did she?"

"She didn't want you to worry while you were at Sunset Palms. She felt bad enough about you having to spend the summer there."

"I liked it there! And my mother treats me like a little kid."

Big Deal lifted her hands helplessly. "She's certainly protective."

Ware looked up at the patient monitor, blank and silent now. It was good news that his grandmother didn't need to prove she was alive anymore, but he still felt terrible. "If I had known, I would have done something, Big Deal. I would have protected you."

"I know you would have, Ware. I know. But your mother . . ." Big Deal fell back against her pillow. "Anyway, look. I'm fine and I have two brand-new hips, and I'll be dancing soon. So it doesn't matter."

But it did.

fifty-nine

"Why didn't you tell me?"

Ware's mother closed her file folder. She looked up, her face puzzled. "Tell you what?"

Ware stood across the table from her. His stomach hurt. "That Big Deal has diabetes."

"Oh. That. There are things a child doesn't need to be bothered with, is all."

"I'm not a child! And I did need to know that. I was staying with her."

She opened her folder again. "Well, I don't see what all the fuss is about, since you're back home."

Ware leaned down and pressed a palm over her papers. "I'm home, but Big Deal isn't. She fell because of her blood sugar. If you'd told me, I could actually have watched her."

Something terrible struck him. "That's what you wished, wasn't it? That first morning I was home, I came down the stairs and heard you and Dad talking. You said you wished something, but Dad said it wasn't what you wanted. You wished you had told me, didn't you?"

His mother looked away. "Of course not. No. Although, in hindsight . . . But it doesn't matter." She pressed a finger to a single tear in the corner of her eye.

That single tear pierced him—not a hundred-arrow volley, maybe only twenty or thirty arrows, it was hard to calculate when you were bleeding—but Ware had to finish. "It matters to me, because it feels like my fault. And it matters to Big Deal. If you had told me, maybe she'd be at home now. Maybe she wouldn't have needed an operation."

She wiped her eye and smiled a tiny smile. "I highly doubt that. She'd been needing those hip replacements for a while."

"Oh. Well, okay. But I'm eleven and a half. If you keep overprotecting me, I'm not going to survive."

"Excuse me?"

"I'm going to get flattened. If I don't start living in the real world, life's going to crush me."

At that, his mother looked so worried about him that Ware grew worried about her.

The checkout lady at the Greek Market had said that things grow into what's needed of them. Ware felt that exact thing happening now. He sat down across from his mother. "I'm not a child, Mom," he said. "You did a good job protecting me, but now I'm strong."

Suddenly, for the first time in his life, Ware knew exactly where he stood. He didn't feel as if he might be wafting, or the slightest bit drifty. He sat up straight in his chair. "I am a person leading a purpose-driven life."

"A purpose-driven life?"

"A purpose-driven life. And the purpose driving it is unfairness." *Thou shalt do battle against unfairness whenever faced with it*—number nine. *Thou shalt be always the champion of the Right and the Good, against Injustice*—number seven. "Unfairness. Injustice. I want to fix it. And I got that from you."

"From me?"

"From you. All day long, you work to fix the worst things that happen, and you love your job."

"You're right," she said after a moment. "Bad stuff happens. I hate that. But I do like fixing it."

"So stop trying to keep bad stuff from me and start teaching me how to fix it."

His mother slid forward on her elbows and rested her chin on her fists. She looked him straight in the eye.

"All right. The first thing is to identify the piece of the problem that you can do something about."

"The piece?"

"You can't fix everything. But . . ." She patted her folder. "Take this morning. A woman came in, desperate because her husband took off, left her with three kids. Her English isn't good and all she has is a part-time housekeeper job. It won't feed three kids. Now, I can't make her husband come back. I can't get her a better job. But I walked her out to the crisis center's food bank, and I signed her up for our night lessons in English. After a while, she'll be okay."

"What if you're just a person, though? What if you don't run a crisis center?"

"Same thing. You identify the piece of the problem you can do something about. Look around the edges—there's always something you can do."

Ware and his mother studied each other across the table for a full minute then, as if they were meeting each other for the first time.

"And Ware," she said at last. "I'm really sorry."

sixty

"Just one more thing before you go up," his mother called from the living room.

Ware paused, one hand on the banister. Since talking with her in the afternoon, he'd been dying to escape into his room so he could think about it all in private.

Ware stepped back into the living room.

"One small thing," she said. "Your grandmother's being released in two weeks."

"Big Deal can go home? Oh, that's great! Why do you and Dad look so worried?"

"She's not quite going home yet," said his father. "First she'll come here for a while. Until she gets adjusted."

"That's really great. I liked living with her. She's

funny and—" Ware stopped. He looked from one parent to the other. "Here? In this house?"

"Yes, Ware," his mother said. "That's what *here* means."

Ware looked around. "But . . . *where* here?"

His father fumbled with his collar. His mother studied her shoes.

And the answer struck him, like a punch to the windpipe. He gulped some air. "You're giving her my room?"

"No, of course not!" his father said. "Never."

And Ware breathed again. Of course not. His parents wouldn't do that to him. They understood.

"She's just had two hip replacements, for heaven's sake," his mother agreed. "She can't be doing stairs. We're giving her our room."

"Oh, good." Ware felt relieved, but a little guilty now, too. He glanced at the couch. It pulled out into a bed, but it was hard and lumpy. "So . . . where will you sleep?"

His father tugged his collar out farther. "We'll be upstairs," he said. "In your room."

"In my . . ." Ware's windpipe closed again. He felt a kick in his gut, too. "The *sofa*? I'm supposed to sleep *here*? Out in the *open*?"

"No. You'll have a room." His mother walked over to the wall of windows and opened the blinds.

The windows looked out onto the back porch.

"What? No!" Ware cried. "It's a porch. It doesn't have any walls!" This was true if by walls you meant places you could lean against or tape up a poster. Places you couldn't see through. Instead, there were windows all the way around: glass on the living room side, clouded plastic on the other three. "It's not a room if it doesn't have walls!"

His mother folded her arms. "Don't worry, I've got it all planned out. There's plenty of room for your bed and your bureau."

"No walls," he moaned.

"It's not forever, Ware," his mother said more kindly. "We'll hang some curtains."

"Athletes train under difficult conditions," his father added weakly. "It makes them stronger."

"We know it's been a disappointing summer," his mother said. "But don't forget, we owe you something nice when it's over."

On that, his parents fled the living room together, as if they'd set a secret timer.

Ware stood alone, realizing with belated shock that he could have argued for hours and all the arguments would be on his side, but none would have worked. He'd lost his room, and he hadn't even gotten a sibling out of the deal.

He pushed open the porch door to see just how bad his life was about to get. Even at nine at night, the summer light lit up every corner of the little space.

He peered outside. Through the hazy plastic, the backyard seemed to be smoking lazily. The shed was a charcoal smudge.

He looked closer. The shed, which they would own in a couple of weeks, had only a single tiny window.

It was an extremely private space. It had a door. He could put a lock on that door.

His parents had promised him something in exchange for his disappointing summer. Well, now he knew what he wanted.

sixty-one

The next day, Ware lay under the queen palms, filming a pair of hawks flying overhead.

For all of third grade, you couldn't go out to recess without some kid asking you which superpower you'd choose: fly or be invisible.

"Invisible," Ware always chose.

"Oh, right," the kid would reply. "So you could spy on people. Cool." Which had shocked him every time. No, he'd never want to spy on people. He just thought it would be nice sometimes to be left alone.

This reminded him of the no-privacy porch he was about to move into.

He put the camera down and rolled onto his side. Jolene was patting some new dandelions into place.

The walkway was lined with flowers now, gold splashes bright as coins.

"Flight or invisbility?" he called over to her.

Jolene sat back and put down her trowel. This was something he liked about her—she thought about questions for a while before answering. "Flight," she decided after a minute, then went to back to her transplanting.

Ware got up and sat beside her. "They look like miniature sunflowers."

Which reminded him of something he'd meant to share with Jolene for a while. Something that would make her laugh, the way she had with Mrs. Stavros.

"That day in the Grotto Bar? You missed it. It was really funny. A woman was sleeping in a booth. Her hair was a perfect circle of yellow, but black in the center. Like a sunflower. That's what I nicknamed her: Sunflower. Get it?"

Instead of laughing, Jolene grew still again. She laced her fingers across her chest and turned to face the Grotto Bar.

Ware tried again. "Or maybe like a halo. A golden halo that was rotten in the middle."

Jolene didn't move.

Ware offered the best detail, his last shot. "I think she was *drunk*."

Jolene got up. She balled up her fists and walked out of the lot.

And Ware felt as if he'd finally gotten his wish—he was invisible. It wasn't so great after all.

sixty-two

Every day after Ashley left, Ware and Jolene jumped into the moat. They swam around where it was deep enough and plowed races where it was shallow. Good luck to any mosquito eggs trying to hatch.

Ware always prepared himself to be reborn when he was in the water, in case a thing like that could surprise you. He never let any hopefulness flicker across his expression, of course.

The water was cool, but the midday, midsummer, mid-Florida sun was too much, even for SPF eighty, hypoallergenic, apply every four hours.

Ware sneaked a sheet out of the laundry basket at home, raided the art closet, and made a banner to string up over the water behind the church.

"What's that in the center?" Jolene asked.

"Coat of arms. It tells people who you are. Mine's a movie camera."

"What's this?" Jolene pointed to the other thing he'd drawn, tiny and in the corner. The thing he'd hoped she wouldn't notice.

"Lizard," he admitted. "That's who I am, too."

Jolene came back the next day with her own sheet. On it, she drew an actual coat with actual arms. The arms were wielding a trowel and a rake, which she sparkled up with a whole jar of glitter. "That's who I am."

Ware pointed to the smaller drawing in the corner.

"Papaya plant. That's who I am, too," she answered.

And Ware saw that she was right. She was feathery and brave at the same time.

Big Deal had said there was a lot he didn't know about Jolene. She said it was never wrong to ask. When a shower popped up after they'd hung the banners, he decided to try *Under the Table*.

"So . . . how come you live with an aunt?" he asked after the candles were lit.

Jolene's eyes narrowed. Ware could practically see the

arrow tips pointing out, but he didn't take cover. "I want to know."

Jolene looked down at her knees. She blew out her bangs. "Okay. But it's nothing, get it? When I was five, my mother put me in the car. There were a lot of suitcases, so I thought we were going on a trip. But we just went around the corner to my aunt's apartment. My mother took me up the stairs along with my suitcase. When my aunt opened the door, my mother dropped my hand and they had a big fight. She said, 'I can't go to Nashville with this.' Walter says I looked like I didn't know what was going on."

"Walter says?"

"He heard the fight and came up."

In the soft drumming of the rain, Ware imagined Jolene as a little girl, holding her mother's hand, all ready for a big trip, and then holding air. It reminded him of the hand-taking episode of their first meeting.

He thought of that hand taking a lot.

Mostly, he wondered how the hand holding had felt to her. He wondered if she ever thought of it at all. He wondered if she'd like someone to hold her hand again.

He edged his right hand out until it almost touched

her left. *Extra information. I didn't hate it when you took my hand,* he practiced in his head until it didn't sound pathetic.

"Oh, good," Jolene said, just as he opened his mouth. "It's stopped raining."

sixty-three

Ware sat at the back doorway, his camera trained on his feet. As he swirled them in the moat water, they seemed to grow longer and bonier, then to slither like fish, and then to lose their toes entirely.

He put down the camera. *Open your eyes. Be a realist,* Jolene had said. She always made it sound as if the real world was solid and reliable, the same for everyone. But for him, it seemed more like his feet underwater. The real world could distort itself. Mess around.

Take his report, for example. The hours had flown by when he was working on it. Then, waiting to get it back, they'd crept along. Seeing the A on the cover, he'd thought the classroom walls seemed to glow, and walking home, gravity loosened its grip.

He looked up. Or take clouds. Scientifically, they were formations of water droplets or ice crystals. But wouldn't three different people looking at them see three different things—a dragon; the promise of rain for papayas; a warning not to take someone's hand?

He looked down. Or take . . .

Ware saw something odd. His leg, above his left knee, was swollen. Had he hit his thigh and not noticed it?

He looked at his other thigh. It had the same firm swelling above the knee. He flexed his legs and laughed out loud.

Muscles!

He flexed his arms. Muscles there, too.

He lifted his shirt. His internal flotation device had deflated.

Of course. In the last few weeks, he could carry a cinder block in each hand without panting. His mother looked at him strangely each night and asked if he was eating enough. Maybe the lot hadn't changed him inside yet, but it had changed him outside. And the outside was part of the inside.

It was a start.

Ware lay back onto the hot foundation. Who was he

kidding? It wasn't a start.

These were the best days he could remember. And the happier he grew, the guiltier he felt, because it was his old self having such a good time. In spite of being in the do-over moat every day, his new self hadn't shown up yet.

It was halfway through August. He needed to try harder.

As soon as Jolene took off that afternoon, he jumped into the water. This time, he would do it right.

"Make me a new person," he said, out loud this time. "Make me a normal kid!" he shouted. He remembered how stirring choir practice had sounded and added a *"Hallelujah!"* for good measure. Then he fell backward.

He held himself underwater and counted off a full minute. He stayed down until his chest hurt. He couldn't tell if this was his new self being born or only his lungs burning from not enough air.

He burst up sputtering and felt the eyes on him before he'd opened his own.

Jolene stood staring from the hedge. She held up her garbage bag. "I forgot this."

Ware froze. Had she heard?

Maybe she hadn't heard.

Of course she had heard.

Jolene put down the bag. Her shoulders rose and fell as if she was sighing over a decision she'd made. She walked down to the moat wall, swung her legs over, and dropped in.

Ware could only watch miserably as she waded up right beside him, probably to deliver a scathing lecture up close about how ridiculous he was.

But he was wrong.

"You can't do it by yourself," she said. "You need someone else to do the dunking."

She cupped his neck with one hand and placed the other between his shoulder blades. "Lean back," she said. "I'll dunk you. But don't ask to be normal. You're already better than that."

sixty-four

The bar was empty. Walter looked up from a book and smiled and said, "Hot one out there," which made Ware's heart slow down and his stomach unclench.

But Walter looked worried, too. "Where's Sprout?"

"Sprout? Oh, right. She's with Mrs. Stavros."

Walter seemed relieved. "The usual?"

Ware nodded—he had a usual now—and took a stool.

Walter set a fresh ginger ale in front of him. He garnished it with a slice of orange that looked tiny in his giant hand. "So, how you doing, pal?" he asked, just as Ware had hoped he would.

Ware took a deep drink and then a deep breath. "Doin' okay, Walter, thanks. But I got this problem."

Walter slid the ChipNutz down the line. Ware shook a handful into his mouth, but only because they were so delicious. He already knew what his problem was. The Knights' Code, number four, demanded: *Thou shalt always speak the truth.* But Ware had not been speaking the truth to his family. Not just about Rec, but about big stuff, like letting them think he was getting normal.

He crunched the ChipNutz thoughtfully. Once again, it helped him clarify his problem.

The clarification was a surprise.

"Walter, I've been lying," he said, "to *myself.*"

"Hoo, boy," Walter said. "Tell me about it."

And Ware did. "Do you ever want to start over, Walter? Like . . . be born again?"

Walter rubbed his neck. "Lord, no. Getting here the one time was hard enough."

"Me either. But all summer I've been telling myself I do. That I want to turn into someone else. But that's not what I want at all."

Walter nodded sympathetically as he polished the already polished bar top.

"What I really want is for it to be okay that I'm *not* someone else."

Walter put the cloth down and stared at Ware hard. "Jolene tells me you're her friend. Being a friend seems like a good place to start with being okay with who you are. Are you her friend, Ware?"

Ware nodded. That's what he was now.

"That's good. So am I. She comes in here, I can watch over her. But when she's out there"—he waved toward the door—"I lose her."

Walter still looked very big, but somehow he also looked small, too. The real world, messing around.

"She's okay with Mrs. Stavros. She feeds her."

"I know that. But she's still pretty alone out there."

"Because she doesn't have her parents."

Walter shook his head. "Leaving a little girl on a door-step like a bag of trash. If I had found that woman . . ."

"You tried?"

"We both did, her aunt and I."

Ware stiffened. "Her aunt helped?"

Walter seemed to read his thoughts. "She was different then. When the church was here. Every Sunday, a fresh start. Tried, anyway. She wasn't always like she is now."

"Everything was something else before," Ware said. "Especially people."

"I guess that's true. Anyway, Jolene has me and Mrs. Stavros. It'd be good if someone else had her back."

Ware sat up so fast his stool swiveled. Here, in this unlikeliest of places, he was being called into service.

He raised his chin, thrust out his chest, and answered boldly. "I've got her back." It was all he could do not to add "My liege lord!" and drop to one knee.

Walter nodded. "You look like someone who means what he says." He leaned forward. "You know, a good watering hole like this brings out people's stories. I've been wondering about you. You got a story, Ware?"

Ware shook his head with regret. "No, I don't have a story."

"Ah, well, you will, pal. Believe me."

sixty-five

Ware put his shovel down to say the very difficult thing. "School starts next Wednesday."

Jolene kicked at some dirt. "For me, too."

Ashley nodded. "Me three."

They stood calculating in silence for a moment.

"Eight days," Ware said.

"Eight days," both girls agreed.

Jolene looked over at the tallest papayas, clustered up with small, hard fruits.

"I have a plan, Jolene," Ware said, hoping his voice didn't shake.

It was a lie, he suddenly saw clearly.

He didn't have a plan. He had five and a half minutes of film and a Magic Fairness Land fantasy. Even if a thousand kids coughed up their allowances, he wouldn't have enough to buy this place. Ten thousand kids.

"Uh-huh." Jolene got up and left for the Greek Market without looking at him. And Ware was grateful for that. He couldn't bear it if he saw himself reflected right now.

Ashley stayed on that afternoon to pick up any litter that could get stuck in a bird's digestive tract, and when Jolene returned after only an hour at the market, they all trudged to the garden to get digging on the newest trench again. Knowing that the work might be futile made it seem tragic, but noble too.

In the middle of the digging, Ware's alarm went off.

"I just heard a warbler," Ashley said, searching the sky. "That's weird. They don't migrate this early."

"Oh, no. Sorry," Ware said. "That's my alarm. I have to go soon."

Ashley looked disappointed, as if she'd really wanted to see a warbler.

"All this stuff you're doing. I hope it helps you," Ware said generously.

"What are you talking about?"

He glanced over at Jolene, then asked Ashley, "This

is for a school project, right? Or to help you get into college?"

"Um . . . no?"

"Then why?"

Ashley planted her spade, walked into the star-shaped
shade of a queen palm, and settled herself down.

Ware followed and dropped into the next star of
shade.

Jolene stayed where she was. But Ware noticed she
cocked an ear up the slope.

"I used to live in Canada?" Ashley began. "We rode
a long way to school on the bus, all these empty roads at
dawn. One day, the bus had to stop because there were
geese all over the road. Highway crews were shoveling
them off. With actual shovels. Their legs were broken.
Some of them were struggling to fly away, but you could
see their legs hanging down all bent and wrong."

Jolene shot a glare up the rise, as though she suspected
Ashley had broken all those goose legs herself.

"We found out afterward. It had rained. In the early-
morning light, the wet highway looked like a river to the
geese. They tried to land on it, and . . ."

Ashley closed her eyes. "I broke my arm once. Bones

are sharp." She stopped and rubbed her right arm, holding it close to her chest. "There must have been two hundred geese, every one with at least one broken bone. All that hurt. How could you measure it?"

Ware didn't answer. Because how could you?

"I decided it wouldn't happen again. Not on my watch. That's why."

Ware looked down at Jolene. He was tempted to say, *See? You were wrong. She just cares about those cranes.* But he didn't. Because he saw that Jolene had already gotten that news and it had about flattened her.

The spade dropped from her hands. She hung her head and Ware saw her take some slow, shaky breaths. Then she walked over to Ashley's shade star and knelt.

"At the end of the night, Walter empties the ChipNutz bowls," she said. "I was thinking, maybe I could save those leftovers for the birds here. I was thinking."

"Sure," Ashley said. "They might like that."

Jolene blew her bangs up. It looked as if she wanted to say something else but didn't know what it was.

"Come here," Ashley told her. "Give me your face." She reached a hand out toward Jolene's cheek.

Jolene startled back. But then she locked her hands

behind her back, closed her eyes, and leaned in. Ware could tell she was holding her breath.

Ashley began tugging her fingers through Jolene's bangs, weaving the shorter hair into the longer hair behind. "I had to grow mine out last year?" she said. "For a while, they're just always in your way."

She looked over at Ware. "She's at a really hard stage right now."

sixty-six

When the car pulled up on First Street the next morning, all three heads turned at the sound. Silently, they laid their tools on the ground and slipped behind the three palm trunks.

After a minute, they saw a man's shape through the mesh on the fencing. The shape moved toward the bright yellow notice, and then the bright yellow notice disappeared.

In its place, the man put up a new notice. It was an even brighter green.

They waited behind the palms until the car drove off. And then, again without talking, the three of them ran down to the fence and climbed over.

The new notice was the same as the old one, except

instead of "Coming This Fall" it read "September 8."

"The day after Labor Day," Ashley said.

That's not even the fall. It isn't fair, Ware wanted to say. But he knew better. He tried to look unconcerned, like a kid with a solid plan B.

Beside him, Jolene started panting in shallow huffs. Then she ran down First Street and vanished into the backyard of the Greek Market.

On his other side, Ashley said, "Public auction. Anyone can bid."

Ware heard a very small click in his brain, like a tiny key trying to pop the lock of a good idea.

He put up his hand so Ashley wouldn't say anything else right now, scare the good idea away.

And in the quiet, it opened up. "Can you come back here tonight?" he asked when he had examined it. "I want to give you a film to give to your father."

Ashley tore off a corner of the auction notice and wrote her number on it. "Call me when you're ready."

When she rode off, Ware stirred up a pot of gluey stucco and began to slather it onto the front of the building. When he had finished catapulting the stucco onto the tower, he found Jolene's rusty knife, sliced a red

261

checkered tablecloth into four flags, and strung one up from each corner of the building. "If an empty lot could become a papaya plantation and a castle, it could become anything," he voice-overed as he filmed the transformed castle.

Then he wrapped himself in the full suit of tinfoil armor, clunked himself down on a cinder block, and beheld.

Wink crawled around from the back of the cinder block. Ware fed him a piece of his apple, and as the turtle chewed, he beheld the church, too—languidly, Ware thought—then turned his wrinkled head. The question he seemed to be asking was *Why?*

"Why not?" Ware answered.

sixty-seven

When Ware got to the lot the next morning, he found Jolene stomping over to her compost piles, a ripped-up papaya plant dangling from each fist.

He ran over. "What are you doing?"

Jolene shot her chin at the auction notice. "I told you before. I won't let the bulldozers crush them. I'll do it myself."

"No, don't!"

She pitched the plants onto the pile and faced him. "Why not? You want to do it yourself? You should. This is all your fault anyway."

"How is it my fault?" Although he knew.

"I should never have listened to you. To your 'I'm

going to save your garden,' all hero-like, all Magic Fairness Land."

She headed back for the garden.

Ware ran over to stand between her and her next victims. "Okay, listen. All the film I've been taking? About the lot, and what we did here? Last night I gave a copy to Ashley to show to her father. She's going to convince him that the city should buy it at the auction. For the community center. I left the Rec a copy today, too. They can build a playground here—no unlit pavement, of course. And a community garden, too. So you can still grow stuff here, Jolene. It's going to be great."

Jolene's eyes grew wide and her jaw fell open. For an instant, the scene spun out in Ware's imagination: she was going to throw her arms around him, she'd be so grateful. He wiped his hands so he could hug her back.

But then she shook her head, as if she were waking up. "It's going to be *nothing*! That's the stupidest idea ever. The only thing stupider is that I trusted you."

"Why? Why is it a stupid idea?"

Jolene threw her arms wide. "Because this is real life. And in real life, bad things happen. Somebody's going to build a strip mall here. Probably have a crappy convenience store, which is actually an *in*convenience store for people like me who might want real stuff, not beer and cigarettes and lottery tickets. If I even get to keep living here, which I won't because I trusted you and didn't get a job, I'm going to have to be all over the trash situation. The customers will pitch their cigarette butts and no-luck lottery tickets in the parking lot, and every night the clerks will throw out the old, wrinkled hot dogs for the rats to fight over. *That's* how the real world works!"

Ware slumped against a queen palm trunk.

He looked down at the papaya plants, feathery and brave at the same time, and over at the shimmering moat, the rocky castle. All their work, and pretty soon it wouldn't exist. "What are we going to do?"

Jolene spun to him, hands on her hips, up in his face. "What are *we* going do? Well, *you* are all set. You always have been. You never needed this place."

She wasn't wearing her sunglasses, but if she had been, Ware knew what he would have seen reflected: a kid who *had* needed this place. All summer, he'd dug rock dust, lugged cinder blocks, built walls, stolen plants, because he'd needed the lot as much as the lot had needed him.

"You never cared."

Ware was shocked. "I *cared*. Inside. In quiet. That's how I am."

Jolene turned around to her plants. She pressed her lips together and headed toward them again.

Ware touched her shoulder. "No. Don't. Just wait and see what happens. It's going to work."

She turned, tears welling in her eyes. And Ware had to thrust his fists into his pockets, the urge to wipe them away was so strong. Had to jam them in, had to punch them in, fists so tight his nails bit into his palms, because otherwise he would have brushed those tears off her cheeks, which Jolene would never have allowed.

She swiped at her cheeks. Her dirty hands smeared a muddy raccoon mask that looked ridiculous and beautiful at the same time, and Ware forced his hands to stay in his pockets, because now he wanted to hold her. What was *wrong* with him?

"Nothing," she spat. "Nothing. Good. Ever. That's the way the real world is. You get that now?"

"It might work," Ware whispered miserably.

She walked out of the lot, head up, shoulders quaking.

Thunk-thunk-thunk.

Ware fetched the bag of plastic letters. **I AM SORRY**, he spelled on the sandwich board sign, both sides.

It didn't begin to cover it.

sixty-eight

That night, Ware's parents wandered from room to room, making a big deal of pinching themselves in disbelief.

"The stairs? We own these beautiful stairs?" one would gasp.

"We own these beautiful stairs!" the other would shout giddily.

"This window, this doorknob, this floor?"

"This window, this doorknob, this floor!"

"We signed the papers this afternoon," Ware's dad explained with a proud grin.

And happiness was like sunshine: It shone on everyone nearby. Ware smiled with his parents, and he meant it. But he had his own weather system going on inside. Dark clouds, cold wind. *Nothing. Good. Ever! That's the way the real world works.*

Yes, he got that now.

In the restaurant, his parents ordered champagne.

Ware picked up the candle in the center of the table and stared into the flame. He would never light the candles *Under the Table* again. Whatever happened with Ashley's father and the auction, his part was over. He would miss every inch of the lot, and every inch of the castle. He would miss the papayas. He would miss the moat. He would miss Wink.

He would miss Jolene.

"Ware." His father touched his arm. "The waiter asked what you'd like to drink."

Ware sighed. "Oh. The usual. Ginger ale, please. With a slice of orange."

He was going to miss Walter and the Grotto Bar.

He dropped his chin to his fists. Above him, his parents clinked their water glasses and grew even sunnier.

"Here's to Labor Day. Working only one shift again

will feel like a vacation," his father said. He turned to Ware. "Maybe school will feel like a vacation to you, huh? After this summer?"

School. He couldn't even imagine a time when he didn't go to the lot. He dropped his head to the table.

All he wanted was for summer not to end.

sixty-nine

Jolene showed up. Ware had worried she wouldn't, but she showed up.

She watered her cans and picked off dead leaves and forked over the compost, but Ware could see that she was only going through the motions. The queen palms shuddered above the row she'd stripped of plants the day before.

Ware patched the moat wall with as much bravado as he could muster, trying to send her the message: He wasn't giving up and neither should she. The city might buy the lot. The city *would* buy the lot. Jolene didn't look like she was receiving the message.

He kept checking the sky for signs of rain. They could talk about it *Under the Table*. The sky grew bluer and brighter every minute.

Finally, he lifted his chin, thrust out his chest, and advanced boldly up the hill. "Are you distraught?" he asked.

Just then, he heard the squeal of bike tires.

Ashley tossed her bike and scaled the fencing. For a moment Ware's hopes rose. But the news he read on her face as she walked toward them crushed them.

"The city isn't going to buy this place?" he asked, but it wasn't really a question.

"There won't even be an auction. It's already been sold. We never had a chance."

"Already sold?" Ware repeated. "That's not . . ." He bit off the word. The last thing he needed was a lecture on Magic Fairness Land.

Ashley hung her head. "Some developers snuck in and cut a deal."

"That's how it works," Jolene said bitterly. "It's going to be a strip mall, isn't it?"

Ashley looked surprised. "Yeah. It's already got tenants signed up."

"Let me guess: a convenience store, right?" Jolene shot Ware a dark look.

"Wow, yeah," Ashley agreed. "And a dry cleaner. And a nail salon, too, I think."

"Perfect." Jolene threw her hands up. "Rat fights, cigarette butts, dry cleaning chemicals to poison us, and who knows what they do with those toenails. Just perfect." She stomped out of the lot, still muttering.

Ware and Ashley watched her climb to her apartment. The stairway shook with each of her steps. Even after she'd slammed the door and Ashley had left, Ware stood rooted, watching where Jolene had disappeared.

A movement in the back window caught his eye. He recognized Jolene's hands even from this distance. They taped a grocery bag over the glass.

Ware climbed the tower and looked down into the pale mirror of the moat. No matter how he turned, he saw himself reflected in the honest water: a kid who had tried to be a hero and failed.

He tore his eyes from the moat and surveyed his kingdom for the last time. Everywhere he looked, he saw unfairness.

And then he looked around the edges.

seventy

When Ware got home, he found his parents bent over the kitchen table, admiring the new deed. "I know what I want," he told them.

His mother looked up. "Hmm?"

"To make up for the summer."

"Oh, good." His dad pulled out his wallet. "Ask away."

"The yard."

"What yard?"

Ware pointed out the back door. "The backyard. And the shed. I want it to be mine."

His father started to laugh, but his mother put a hand on his shoulder and shook her head. "Cyrus told me you might ask for the yard. Of course it's yours. I have a feeling you'll turn it into something amazing."

Ware went outside and stood on the back step. The yard looked exactly the same as it had all summer—a wasteland. But it looked entirely different, too—trembling with hopeful excitement. The real world, messing around again.

Then he went back inside. He picked up the phone and dialed. "Do you miss digging?" he asked when Ashley answered.

"That's so weird," she said. "I kind of do?"

seventy-one

Ware stood on the community center doorstep. He could bear it for this one last day. Then he'd retrieve his father's first aid kit and go say goodbye to the lot.

Saying goodbye to the lot would be even harder, but he could do that, too, because after that, he'd get to tell Jolene what he'd done.

He lifted his chin, thrust out his chest, and opened the door boldly.

But inside, fifty kids were running around and shouting, and his soul shrank down behind his heart. Maybe he'd go float in the moat all day. Maybe he'd lie under the queen palms and watch clouds.

He slipped over to the cubbies, pulled the first aid kit from the back, and hurried toward the door.

Ms. Sanchez caught him before he could escape. "I was hoping I'd see you," she said. "Ware, right?"

"Uh . . . we . . . it turned out I didn't need to . . ."

Ms. Sanchez waved a hand. "It happens. But I wanted to tell you that I saw that film you made. Very impressive."

"Oh. Thanks. It didn't work, though. The community center isn't going to get the lot."

She shrugged. "No, and that's a shame. But I was thinking something else."

Suddenly, she didn't look quite so tired. "We have a big screen we use for movie nights, once a month. What a waste, I was thinking. Here we have a young man who knows his way around a camera. How would you feel about starting a film club?"

"Me? But, I'm not a professional or anything."

"Do you know what the word amateur means, Ware?"

Ware shook his head.

"It means 'someone who loves something.' I think that's what we need here. I could round up a couple of used movie cameras. You and any interested kids could teach each other."

Ware's soul uncurled a little bit. "You'd really let me do that? Because I could do that." Just then, a Wiffle ball bashed his shoulder.

He picked it up and looked across the room.

He saw, just like he had his first day, a huge space filled with kids. Some in big groups, some in small ones, a few alone. The outside was part of the inside when it was people.

He had no idea who might want to join a film club. But he knew where he wanted to start.

"Hey, Ben!" he called to the tall-necked boy, who was painting at an easel, then tossed the ball.

Ben caught it and trotted over.

"Do you like movies?" Ware asked.

seventy-two

"One hundred fourteen plants! Who would do that? Someone terrible, that's who. Probably that bank guy, with the suit. And the compost! That's the worst! All that work, me and the worms!"

Ware wished he had his camera. For five minutes Jolene had been ranting at full throttle, and he would have filmed every second. Even now, winding down, the sheer power and the glory of her indignation made you want to stand up and cheer.

But of course, she didn't know.

"Jolene, that's not—"

"No, the worst is Mrs. Stavros's shopping cart! She trusted me and now I have to tell her I let it get stolen."

Ware shot his palms out, policeman style. "Stop. Listen!"

"Nope! Don't even start with some stupid story from Magic Fairness Land. Because here in the real world, bad stuff happens. People steal shopping carts and compost and little plants."

Ware saw Jolene was intent on seething for a while longer. And somehow, he didn't want to tell her what he'd done anymore. He wanted her to see it.

"Fine, no story," he said. "Follow me."

"Where?"

"Follow me."

"Why?"

"Because I say so. One time, *you* follow *me*."

Jolene refused to walk with him, and he heard her stewing darkly behind him the entire hour it took to get there. When they finally reached his driveway, he wasn't so sure he'd done the right thing.

Jolene drew up. "You live here?"

"Yes. But that's not what—"

"The whole house? You own it?"

"Well, since last week. But—"

"And you can never get kicked out? You're so lucky."

Ware turned to his house. He saw it as if for the first time. A whole house. From the wide front step he used to jump off for hours when he was five to his room tucked under the eaves where the skylight above his bed perfectly framed the Big Dipper each January, which he would have to give up next week but would get back in a couple of months. And everything in between.

"You're right," he said. "I am. But—"

"Great. Well, thanks for showing me how lucky you are. Now I'm going to walk back and tell Mrs. Stavros that I lost her shopping cart." She spun toward the sidewalk.

Ware almost lunged for Jolene's hand to pull her back, but he caught himself at the last second. "I took it," he said instead, shoving his hands into his pockets. "That's what I'm trying to tell you. The shopping cart. It's here."

"Right, sure." Jolene scowled, but she followed him to the backyard.

For a good ten seconds, she stood frozen, like a stop-motion frame. And then she fell on her knees in front of the ChipNutz cans and brushed her fingertips over the papaya plants, looking as if she wanted to hug each one. "They're all here? All hundred fourteen?"

"All hundred fourteen."

She ran to the compost piles, turned to him.

"Ashley helped. And your tools are in the shed."

"All this . . . ?"

Ware joined her. "It's yours. You'll have to start over, but I'll help."

"It's mine?"

"My parents gave it to me, and I'm giving it to you."

She pointed to the sandwich board. "'The Real World,'" she read out loud, her eyebrows lifted into questions.

"Because you're right. Bad stuff happens. But the real world is also all the things we do about the bad stuff. We're the real world, too."

Jolene took off her sunglasses. And in her eyes, Ware saw himself reflected. A kid who was maybe a little bit of an actual hero.

seventy-three

When Ware heard the car drive in at five, he raised a thumb to Jolene. He had prepared for everything.

A few seconds later, his mother stepped out the back door. "No more second shifts!" she said with a dramatic hand thrown over her forehead. She looked around. "What's all this?"

"You gave me the backyard," Ware reminded her.

"Of course. But I wasn't expecting . . ."

"Papayas!" Ware launched into his speech. "Jolene says we can have as many as we want."

His mother seemed to notice Jolene for the first time. A smile blossomed on her face. "Jolene?"

"My friend from this summer. Now, papayas are good for breakfast, lunch, or dinner."

His mother's smile grew broader. "Your *friend*. How nice. From the Rec."

Too late, Ware saw that actually, he had *not* prepared for everything. He had omitted a crucial detail. He tried to signal Jolene, but she had already dropped her shovel and was brushing off her hands.

"No, ma'am," she said, all sweet politeness. "I met Ware at the lot."

"Papayas," Ware tried, "are excellent in smoothies!"

"At the lot?" his mother asked, ignoring the diversion.

Jolene nodded. "Right. After he quit Rec."

Ware stepped between them. "They're loaded with vitamins. *Vitamins*, Mom!"

His mother leaned around him. "After he . . . excuse me? *Quit Rec?*"

"Yes. You know," Jolene said, sounding a little nervous now. "When we built the moat? You know. Ma'am."

"The moat? I know . . . ?" Ware's mother pinched the bridge of her nose. She raised her other hand, as if asking the world to slow down. "You come inside, Ware. We're going to have a conversation." Then she disappeared, shaking her head.

Ware and Jolene darted to the picnic table. The crossbars cramped the space. Still, *Under the Table* was the right place for a huddle.

"You said they didn't care," Jolene hissed. "You said they were happy you weren't alone and had stuff to do. You said they didn't care."

"I meant they *wouldn't* care. If they knew, they wouldn't care."

"Well, extra information: your mother cares."

seventy-four

"I think you should tell me about your summer." Ware's mother drummed the table. Her voice was oddly calm, but dangerously high-pitched. "Apparently I missed something."

"Okay, sure," Ware said. "My summer. Well . . ." He pulled the Rec brochure from the refrigerator door and consulted its offerings. "I had many Diverse Enrichment Opportunities and built my Real-Life Skills. I made a stained-glass window. I learned how to grow things and built a moat. You should see all the birds that came. I stopped going to Rec. My summer was great!"

"Excuse me?"

"I said my summer was great."

"Not that part." His mother leaned in and cupped her ear. "About you not going to Rec."

"Well, right, I had all those valuable experiences *instead* of Rec. And my summer *was* great. I made a film with Uncle Cy's camera. And the film went—"

"Not once? Every day all summer I dropped you off, and you . . . you never went inside?"

"Of course I went inside. A few times. In the beginning. And I brought the film to the Rec. That's what I'm trying to tell—"

"Over five hundred dollars, and you skipped?"

"I offered to pay you. Twice as much, remember? You would have *made* money!"

She couldn't argue that point, but Ware could see she was regrouping for a side-flank assault. He seized the advantage. "I had Meaningful Social Interactions every day, just like you wanted. With other kids, with Walter, with—"

"Who is Walter?"

"So . . ." He shouldn't have mentioned Walter. "You'd like him. He listens to people and helps them solve their problems." He edged the Rec brochure across the table.

"And now Ms. Sanchez wants me to—"

"I don't think I know a social worker named Walter. Where did you say he practices?"

Why had he mentioned Walter? "Uh . . . near the community center. And here's the best part: I'm going back to Rec. Ms. Sanchez invited me. And this time you don't have to pay!"

That threw her off the Walter track, at least. "No? How's that?"

Ware explained about the film club. When he finished, he dropped his shoulders and spread his arms wide. "That's all I've got, Mom. I'm trying to be normal, but this is as close as I get."

"What do you mean, trying to be normal?"

"I know you wish you had a normal kid." He felt a dangerous prick behind his eyes. "I heard you."

"I would never say something like that."

"The first day of Rec. You told Dad that I tried to buy my way out of it. You called me antisocial."

"What? No. You misheard."

"I didn't mishear. You asked Dad, 'Why can't we have a normal kid?'"

"I said that?" Her eyes filled. "I was so stressed then. With your grandmother, with the extra shifts. It's not an excuse—I should never have said that. I didn't mean it, and I'm so sorry you heard it." She wiped the tears from her eyes and leaned back. "All the time, I was protecting you so you wouldn't get hurt—I know, I know, *overpro-*tecting you!—and it turns out I'm the one who . . ." She got up and wrapped her arms around him. For a moment, relief flooded through him.

"I've only ever wanted you to be happy."

He pulled away. "But I'm not you, Mom. Sometimes I'm happy doing stuff by myself. Uncle Cy says he's that way, too. He says being like that is normal. For an artist."

"Cyrus was trying to tell me that. I think I was trying not to listen." She picked up the Rec brochure, tore it in half, and threw the pieces in the trash.

Just then, Ware's dad's walked in the front door. Ware held his head in his hands as he listened to his mother tell him what she'd just learned.

"Let me get this right, son," his dad said when he'd heard the whole thing. "You asked for the backyard, just to give it away?"

Ware looked up. His dad wore the baffled, cotton-ball expression again. He hung his head and nodded.

"Your big reward for the summer, which your mother said seemed really important to you. You just gave it away?"

Ware's head sank to his chest. He spread his hands in apology. "Jolene needed it more."

His dad wrapped an arm around Ware's shoulder and squeezed. "You're a real team player," he said. "I am so proud of you."

His mother rose. "I think you ought to show us this film that got so much attention."

Ware sat between his parents and opened the film. While it ran—six minutes and three seconds—he watched their eyes. For six minutes and three seconds they never left the screen.

At the end, his mom sat quietly for a minute. "I think Cyrus is right."

Ware felt himself swell. "You think I'm an artist?"

"That, of course," she said. "But I meant he's right that it makes us lucky."

Late that night, after they'd gone for pizza and shopped for a thousand things for school, which did include black jeans and a black T-shirt but did not include ear piercing, Ware lay in bed looking up at the ceiling plaster whorls. Tonight they looked like smiles on top of smiles inside smiles.

seventy-five

Jolene took the three-forty-five bus to Ware's house every day after school, bringing along a garbage bag full of old fruit and vegetables from the Greek Market, and took the five-ten bus home.

One day, she stayed a little later than usual. They were inside drinking lemonade when Ware's mother came in from the living room.

"I notice there's a pile of garbage out back" was the first thing she said.

Ware hurried to intercede. "We'll move it behind the shed. Or cover it."

His mother gave him a puzzled look, then smiled at Jolene. "We'll start saving our scraps for your compost. I'll leave them in a can by the back door."

"Your *scraps*? You'll give me your *scraps*?" Jolene asked, the way a normal person might ask, "Your *gold*? You'll give me your *gold*?" Then she had to say, "Thank you, ma'am" about a dozen times, until finally Ware went to the door and nodded meaningfully to the waiting garden.

But his mother wasn't finished. "You know, people drop produce off at the food pantry. Sometimes it's past its prime, and we have to throw it out. I'll bring it home from now on, add it to the pile."

Jolene about fell on her knees thanking her for that.

"We should get back outside," Ware tried.

But his mother held up a finger. She opened the drawer under the desk and drew out the fresh red school-year planner she'd bought for Ware. Each morning, she'd left it by his backpack, and each morning he'd put it back in the drawer.

He groaned. "Mom, she doesn't want—"

His mother waved him off. She flipped open the planner in front of Jolene. "There's a calendar up front. We can mark planting dates, harvest dates—things like that. There's a section for notes and see, here in the back, there's a spreadsheet. We'll keep track of what you get per pound, profit and expenses."

Ware tried to catch Jolene's eye, to mime to her that she could just ditch the planner. But Jolene lifted it as reverently as if it were sewn together of butterfly wings. "We?" she asked. "You'll *help* me? And I can *keep* this?"

And Ware realized: He had just gotten his sibling wish. Half of it, anyway.

Just then, Ware's father stuck his head in from the living room, smiling in pride. "Garbage, a planner, and some help," he confirmed what his miracle of a wife had organized. "A hat trick."

Jolene spun to him, clutching the planner to her chest. "You know *hockey*?" she asked, breathless with hope.

Ware's dad clapped his hands together and rubbed them. "The season opener is in three weeks. Save you a spot on the couch?"

seventy-six

Jolene didn't change the message on the sandwich board, even after Ware showed her the bag of letters in the shed. He'd also told her she could get rid of the picnic table, make room for more plants, but she'd kept that, too. Crouched *Under the Table*, knees touching, they said whatever had to be said.

"Walter got the bill," Jolene said the first time. "Apparently water's not free."

"So . . . do we have to pay him back?"

Jolene laughed, a thing she did so often now Ware was getting used to the sound. "He says I have to flatten boxes for him for the rest of my life. He says you have to help, too."

It took Ware another week to get up the courage to

ask what had to be asked. "Did they clear the lot?" He wrapped his arms, bracing himself.

"Nope. They worked in the front for a couple of days, but then the police came and made them stop."

Ware straightened so fast he hit his head. "The police? How come?"

"Wink."

"Sir Wink? The turtle?"

"Nuh-uh. Tortoise. Apparently, Wink is a gopher tortoise."

"Well, so?"

"So Ashley showed your film to her Audubon group. One of the bird ladies jumped off the couch when she saw Wink and shouted, 'Whoa, whoa, hold it right there, that's a gopher tortoise!' The good thing about them is they're on the threatened and endangered species list."

"How is that good?"

"Well, it's not good for Wink, obviously. But it meant they had to stop clearing the lot until they could get a wildlife expert to come out. The bulldozer guy was not happy."

"Wow. So . . . maybe the lot could be a refuge. Maybe the community center could still have some of it." He would rename his film *Saved by a Tortoise*. They could—

"Nope. Still here in the real world, remember? It took a while to get someone there—these wildlife experts, pretty busy, I guess. Anyway, they're going to 'relocate' Wink next week. Then they'll have to find his burrow and protect that, since hundreds of other species camp out in gopher tortoise burrows, too. That will take a while. It didn't save the lot, though. Eventually, they'll clear it. But still."

But still. Uncle Cy had been right. You never knew who would see your film, or what would happen when they did.

"I heard about the lady recognizing Wink," Ware said when Ashley answered her phone. "Any other things they mentioned about my film?"

"They liked the bird parts best, of course," Ashley said. "They loved the parakeets in the palms."

"But about my filming? More about that?"

"No, sorry. Except Mrs. Watson said, 'That boy sure likes that girl's hands' about a dozen times. They all laughed about that."

"Okay, never mind. Tell me about the lady who recognized Wink. All the details."

"Well, um . . . she's pretty old? I never saw her move like that before. She jumped right off the couch. We were all kind of worried about her."

"I mean, tell me what she said about me."

"Oh. She couldn't believe you were only eleven."

"I'm eleven and a half. No, wait. Eleven and three-quarters."

"She kept saying, 'He's only eleven? That young man is going somewhere!'"

"Eleven and three-quarters. Did she say where? Where I was going?" Over the phone, Ware imagined Ashley recalling a list of exotic places: Morocco, Hong Kong, Calcutta. Somehow the twirling sounded as if she was recalling a long list of exotic places. Morocco, Hong Kong, Calcutta. Because kids like him turned into grown-up filmmakers like his uncle.

"No," she said. "Just 'somewhere.' 'That young man is going somewhere. And he's only eleven,' she kept saying."

Ware sighed. "And three-quarters."

Then he gave Ashley his number. "Call me if you

remember anything else the Audubon ladies said. You can call me anytime."

"Um . . . I think I remembered everything already?"

"Just in case," he said. "Anytime."

seventy-seven

Two months later, on a Sunday afternoon when his whole family had gathered for Big Deal's birthday, Ashley did call. "The cranes are on their way." She was so excited she didn't even turn it into a question. "Let's watch from the lot."

Um . . . *YES?!*

He ran to the living room. "Come to the lot at seven. I have a surprise," he told everyone.

"I'll bring my camera," his uncle said.

Big Deal winked. "Will the little skulker be there?"

Unbelievable. His own grandmother.

"I'm going to get her now," he called, and then he took off on his bike. He pulled up in front of the Grotto Bar, panting. He could really use the usual—maybe a double—but he headed straight up the stairs to Jolene's apartment and banged on the door.

Catching his breath on the landing, he looked down over the lot. The moat was only half full now, and suspiciously green, but it glinted in a contented manner.

On Friday, Jolene had told him the wildlife people had finished protecting Wink's burrow. The bulldozers were coming back Monday to finish.

Monday, *tomorrow*. Tomorrow they'd smash the walls, spill the water, scrape the land to bone.

The thought made his chest hurt. He was grateful when he heard steps shuffling to the door.

The woman who opened it had the yellowest hair he'd ever seen. It sprang out of her head like a crown. The center was black.

A bunch of answers fell into place, none of them good. He remembered the worried look on Walter's face as he scanned the booths, and how he'd sent Jolene away. The things Jolene had said about her aunt. He remembered how her face had hardened when he'd joked about Sunflower's name, and about how maybe she'd been drunk.

Ware felt his face redden. How mean he must have

sounded. How much wanton offense he had given.

Jolene came sliding into the hall. She dashed past Ware onto the landing into the neon light flashing from the endlessly thirsty flamingo.

"I'm sorry," Ware whispered.

"I know." She sighed. "Me too."

seventy-eight

"They looked like saints coming up the drawbridge," Ware voice-overed as he filmed.

It wasn't his imagination, either—the visitors all did look like saints. First, because a camera lens reveals how special people are, even people who appear ordinary. Also, because the streetlight above made halos around their heads. Ware had scooped a case of light sticks from his father's truck, so the drawbridge glowed like a runway, lighting people mysteriously from below, too.

Ashley arrived first with her father and eight Audubon ladies. Ware filmed her helping the oldest one settle onto the pew as gently as if the woman were a fragile bird she was tucking into a nest. He put down the camera and went over and introduced himself. "I'm almost twelve," he told the couch jumper. "Practically twelve."

Next up came his family. His parents guided Big Deal by the elbows, although she kept batting their hands away. Uncle Cy followed, arms outspread to catch her if she fell. Besides the streetlight halos and the light sticks, they all seemed to be glowing from inside, too.

Ware's mother paused in front of the Audubon ladies as she squeezed by them on the pew. "Did you see the film? My son made that film. My son, Ware. I'm his mother," she said to each.

The first time Ware heard it, he about fell into the moat. After he heard it the second time, he trained his camera on her, to preserve the extraordinary event in case she said it again. But when she did say it a third time, he put the camera down. Because it turned out he didn't want anything between them when his mother's face lit up with pride.

When she sat down beside Big Deal, he picked up the camera again and panned it over to Jolene. She had gone to say a final goodbye to her garden and found a ripe fruit. She twisted it off and bundled it in her sweatshirt like a baby. As she carried it up the drawbridge, he saw how special she was, too. How there wasn't another person like her.

He stopped her as she passed him. "Do you want to get your aunt?"

Jolene shook her head and pointed to the back driveway. "Here comes my person." She laid the papaya baby on the rim of the baptistery and ran down to take a jug of juice from Mrs. Stavros and help her up the drawbridge.

Ware fetched a stack of communion cups and doled them out. He lit candles for the holders on the pew and then filmed Mrs. Stavros passing her jug down the row, and the people filling the tiny cups as they introduced themselves. His stained-glass window reflected the candles in little jewel-y flickers.

Ware hung his camera around his neck and joined Jolene at the other end of the pew. "How come you never let me go to the Greek Market with you?"

Jolene raised her eyes to the side fence. "She's going to leave it to me when she goes back to Greece."

"Well, that's great. But why couldn't I go with you?"

Jolene looked over at Mrs. Stavros, refilling Uncle Cy's cup. She hung her head. "Because she's my saint. I was afraid I might lose her."

"You could lose her if I went over there?"

"I'm her favorite person in the whole world. Nobody

else likes me best. I was afraid if she met you, she might like you better."

Ware sat a moment, searching for the words to tell her he would never have let that happen. Before he could find them, Ashley's phone buzzed.

She looked down at it and then held up a hand. "They just flew over Tuscawilla Lake," she announced. "They're ten minutes away."

Just then, Walter came hustling across the lot clutching a flashlight and a can of ChipNutz. Ware turned the camera on. Through the lens, he looked like a saint, too, but then Walter looked like a saint all the time.

Walter gave Jolene a kiss on the head and patted Ware's shoulder. "You've got yourself a story now, pal," he said.

Ashley held up her hand again. "Two minutes."

The crowd grew still.

Ware folded his hands on his lap and looked up. The rising moon was almost full behind the clouds, the sky deep violet. He remembered a twilight like this at the beginning of the summer, when he had lain at the bottom of a pool, watching a bird carve the sky, wishing for someone to share the sight.

They heard the cranes first, trumpeting their prehistoric cries.

Ware lifted the camera to the north sky, and then there they were—a hundred, two hundred, a thousand and more. Wave after wave, printing the sky like live hieroglyphs. The air thumped with the beat of their wings and the three queen palms fluttered skyward, raising their fronds in praise.

Ware stood. He slipped out of the pew and over to the back of the foundation, still filming. He panned the camera down over the moat, and as he did, the moon emerged and the water flashed silver, reflecting the flight of the birds.

And himself.

Ware felt as if he had climbed the world's tallest watchtower, because suddenly he could see the whole picture.

He saw that Walter was right—he had himself a story now. But it wasn't just his story; it was the story of the cranes and the story of the lot and it was Jolene's story, too, and Ashley's, and the story of everyone gathered here tonight, because all their stories were one.

Suddenly Jolene was beside him. Without thinking,

Ware let his free hand reach out and find hers. He held his breath.

Jolene curled her fingers around his and squeezed. And then she said exactly what he was thinking. "*Now* this place is holy."

Ware squeezed back. He trained the camera on the last of the cranes. He knew how those birds felt, those birds beating their way home just as they had for millions of years, to a place that always let them land softly. Ware knew exactly how they felt, because at that moment, he had wings.

"You see that?" he asked. Not in his head, not in a whisper, but in a voice that everyone heard. "Wow."

A boy. A fox.
A search for home.

"You going back for your home or your pet?"
"They're the same thing."